I0727116

The Innkeeper's Unwelcome Winter Bride

Cheryl Wright

Copyright

THE INNKEEPER'S UNWELCOME WINTER BRIDE
(Unwelcome Brides Series – Book Nine)

Copyright ©2025 by Cheryl Wright

Small Town Romance Publications

All rights reserved. Without limiting the rights under copyright reserved above, no part of this publication may be reproduced, stored in or introduced into a retrieval system, or transmitted, in any form, or by any means (electronic, mechanical, photocopying, recording, or otherwise) without the prior written permission of the copyright owner of this book.

This is a work of fiction. Characters, places, and incidents are a figment of the author's imagination. Any resemblance to actual events, locales, organizations or people living or dead, is totally coincidental.

- This book was written by a human and not Artificial Intelligence (A.I.).
- This book cannot be used to train Artificial Intelligence (A.I.).

Dedication

To Margaret Tanner, my very dear friend and fellow author, for her enduring encouragement and friendship.

To Alan, my husband of over fifty years, who has been a relentless supporter of my writing and dreams for many years.

To You, my wonderful readers, who encourage me to continue writing these stories. It is such a joy knowing so many of you enjoy reading my stories as much as I love writing them for you.

Table of Contents

Chapter One

Helena, Montana – 1880s

Elizabeth Dunagan crouched low at the back of the stall.

She fought hard to ignore the agitation her presence brought to the horse whose stall she had hidden in.

She tried her best to control her breathing, willing herself to calm down. The more anxious she became, the more agitated the gelding became. Lizzie peered through the crack in the door to the stall.

Two men made their way through the livery, checking each stall. The sound of the horses seemed to get louder by the minute. It was no longer only her horse agitating, but the others now joined him.

Her heart pounded, sweat poured down her face. The men were now close.

Was this the end of her?

As the door to the stall began to open, the gelding reared up. He seemed to sense the danger these men represented to Lizzie. He had always protected her, even when she was a young child. It broke Lizzie's heart to see her childhood horse locked up like this – he needed freedom, to run, and to feel the wind on his face.

His constant kicking and agitation didn't seem to deter the men. Despite the obvious threat the gelding signified, they continued to try to enter the stall. Big John was having none of it.

"Damned horse," the man growled, then pulled the door closed again.

Lizzie heard a grunt. It seemed to come from the second killer. "At least we know she's not in there," he said. "That is one angry animal. He's not at all friendly. No one could survive in there."

Lizzie held her breath, hoping the first man agreed. If he didn't, she was in for a whole lot of trouble.

As if the crisis she was dealing with now was not enough.

Lizzie finally felt comfortable leaving the haven she'd claimed in the livery, despite the daylight. The two men had long gone, and all was quiet. At least it appeared that way.

She couldn't stay in the livery forever – she would eventually be found if she did.

That she'd witnessed their murderous spree meant she was a target for these unscrupulous bank robbers. There was no need for them to kill anyone – the bank manager complied and opened the safe as they instructed.

After claiming everything of value, they'd herded everyone inside the safe, promising to leave them in peace.

Lizzie was in the wrong place at the wrong time.

She should have known something was wrong – the *closed* sign on the door to the bank was visible, yet it was early in the day. Her mind was full of confusion and uncertainty as she continued inside.

Standing at the bottom of the stairs, her mind in chaos, Lizzie glanced about. It was only then her confusion cleared. The bank was being robbed. Her heart pounded as the robbers suddenly opened fire on their victims. Everything seemed to happen in slow motion.

To stifle a scream, and to cover her presence, Lizzie stuffed her fist in her mouth. Then she did the unthinkable, she turned in their direction. They saw her! She had to get away!

It appeared Lizzie was the only living witness. A shiver went through her. If the bank manager hadn't asked her to run an errand for him, she too, would have been in that safe. She would also be lying dead on the floor with the others.

As the manager's assistant, she often had to do certain errands for him. To Lizzie, it was the worst part of her job. Only today, it saved her life.

Lizzie knew she would have been next had she hesitated, even for a few seconds. She ran as fast as her short legs would take her.

With no idea where she was running too, Lizzie's brain was in overdrive. Where should she hide? She could run to the sheriff's office, except the sheriff was out of town today. Any other day his office would have been a safe haven.

Could she risk going there? The sheriff's deputy may happen to be there. It was then Lizzie remembered the deputy was only recently appointed to his position. He was not experienced, which could mean they would both be killed. She had no intention of putting the deputy's life at risk to save her own.

In her heart, Lizzie wished the bank manager and his staff were fine. Were alive. Except her eyes proved otherwise. Shot multiple times, they had no chance of survival.

She headed to the only building with any sign of life, somewhere other people were most likely to be found. Where she could blend in, perhaps?

Still running, breathing heavily, trying to catch her breath, Lizzie ran inside the nearest building showing any signs of life. If it wasn't for the clerk standing behind the counter, Lizzie may have thought the place deserted. He fiddled about with keys, his back to her. He seemed to be sorting room keys. Lizzie didn't have the time to stop and find out.

She sprinted up the elegant staircase, looking for somewhere to hide. All the time praying the innkeeper didn't turn around and see her.

Slowing down the moment she reached the top of the stairs, Lizzie frantically glanced about. A trolley filled with towels, sheets, and pillowcases. Outside a room, and the door was open.

Should she hide in there? Could she conceal herself enough to stay safe?

Lizzie crept forward, silently making her way into the vacant room. She heard movement in the small bathroom. She'd heard this place was high class, now she knew it for fact.

She likely had only moments to get her bearings and find a hiding place.

Still, she couldn't help but glance about. This room was like no other room she'd seen before. This room, the interior, the bed, and the way it was decorated, screamed sophistication.

This was no ordinary room.

Lizzie softly dropped to the floor. She wriggled about until she was under the bed and out of sight.

She couldn't see the maid, or the room she worked in, and wondered how many rooms of this caliber the inn had. Not many, she was certain. There wouldn't be many guests requiring such a room. As such, she deemed it a safe place for her to hide. At least for now.

She heard the maid moving about and humming, the sound getting ever closer. Lizzie squeezed herself further under the bed and held her breath. She could not be found – Lizzie was certain if her presence was known, she would be forced to leave. If that happened, it was like signing her own death certificate.

Those killers would stop at nothing to eliminate her – the only witness to their murderous actions at the bank.

Chapter Two

Charles Lovett finally finished sorting the keys. This was not a task he normally undertook, but with his receptionist ill, he had to take over.

It was not an undertaking he enjoyed. His job was to run the business side of the inn – Charles enjoyed the challenge of keeping the books up to date and accurate.

He expected high standards from his staff, including the maids, the kitchen staff, and the wait staff.

He inherited the inn from his uncle – his father's brother. It had surprised Charles as he hadn't seen Uncle Jeremy for several years. Not since his wife, Aunt Meredith had passed.

Jeremy's lawyer informed Charles the inn was a viable business, and he was intrigued by the opportunity.

After selling his accounting business in New York, he set off for Montana with high hopes for the future. What he found was depressing. The interior was old and run down. Instead of closing the inn, Charles decided to sell it.

Several months later, he conceded the state it was in meant the inn would never sell. He had to change his way of thinking.

Instead of walking away, as he'd contemplated, Charles decided to transform the inn. To make it the sort of place only the wealthy would visit. He hired tradesmen to renovate the entire building. Even the owner's private quarters was run down.

After months of work, and far more money than he anticipated, the new inn was finally ready. Instead of a rundown eyesore of a building, he had a sophisticated, high-class inn. He priced the rooms accordingly.

Of course, there would be times the inn was quiet, and sometimes he questioned his decision to make it such a sophisticated place. If it was of a lower standard, he would surely have more guests, but the price would also have to be far lower.

Charles shook his head.

Why he even entertained such thoughts, he didn't know. The inn's restaurant was kept busy quite often with travelers. They were not afraid to part with their money to get a decent home cooked meal. It wasn't like the restaurant was always full, because it wasn't, but the number of guests who frequented the restaurant meant the costs for staff and food was always covered.

He was relatively happy with that particular outcome. Even if he did only break even. On the other hand, there were days when the restaurant was full, and he had to send potential customers away as he had to give preference to the guests staying at the inn. It really cut him to the core having to do it. One thing Charles did not like was refusing good money.

There were times he wished the dining room was larger, but other times he wished it smaller. No matter what he did, Charles knew he couldn't win.

"Mr. Lovett," one of the maids shouted frantically as she ran down the stairs. "Come quickly!"

Charles glanced toward the young woman he'd recently hired. She was breathless, and white as a ghost.

"Whatever is wrong?" he asked. He studied her — she was petrified. By what, he didn't know.

"There's a 'truder," she whispered once she was close to him. Why on earth she chose now to lower her voice, Charles would never know. Thankfully, there were no guests around, as they had already checked out.

"Bessie," he said gently. "Sit down and take a breath."

The young woman stared at him, then sat, her eyes filling with tears. She sat quietly for what seemed a long time, but Charles knew it was only due to her anxiety regarding what had occurred. "Should I get tea?" he asked. Didn't tea fix everything? His mother always partook of tea during the most difficult times.

Bessie shook her head, then wiped at her eyes. "I…I saw a foot 'truding out from under the bed," she said. "Room," she had to think then. Charles waited patiently. "Room sixteen." She closed her eyes and thought. "No, 'twas fifteen." She brought a hand to her face and brushed back her stray hair. "I just come out of the bathroom, Sir, and there it was – the foot. I don't know if it 'twas dead or 'live, Sir, but the foot 'twas there, stickin' out like it belonged." Her breath came out in a whoosh then, and Charles realized how truly distraught she was.

He watched the young woman for a minute, until the cook walked nearby. "Martha," Charles said, calling across the room. "Look after Bessie, will you? She's had a fright. There's apparently an intruder in room fifteen."

Martha stared at him. "An intruder? Oh my. Come with me, girl," she said gently, and headed toward the kitchen with Bessie beside her.

Charles headed up the grand staircase. His heart pounded harder with every step he took. He convinced himself the young maid was delusional. It would be the best outcome for all concerned.

He could understand how someone could slip into one of the rooms at the inn unseen. With the hustle and bustle of check out, it would be quite easy to get past the staff. Except today he was manning the front desk. They must have slipped past while he sorted the keys. There was no other explanation.

The question he asked himself was *why*? Why would anyone want to install themselves into one of the inn's rooms? They would soon be found and removed.

After finally reaching the top of the stairs, Charles braced himself. What he would find, he had no idea. If it was a dead body, how did it get there? If it was a living person, he would have to deal with the trespasser and get the sheriff involved. Either way, he wasn't looking forward to entering the room.

It was then Charles realized he carried no weapon. He rarely wore firearms, but today wished he did. He stood outside room fifteen as he pondered the situation. He didn't employ security – he'd never found it necessary. He did have male porters. They were expected in an establishment such as his.

Charles rubbed a hand through his hair. Should he go back downstairs and get one of the porters for backup? Except they were mere boys, barely men.

What use would they be in a difficult situation such as this?

Finally deciding to enter the room alone, Charles pushed the door open. An unpleasant smell hit him. Surely it wasn't what he thought? The pungent aroma reminded him of horse manure. He couldn't stop himself from grimacing.

Glancing about, he tried to find the foot Bessie had worried over. Except he saw nothing out of place. If it hadn't been for the repulsive odor, he would believe Bessie had imagined anyone, or indeed, anything, being in the room.

Charles cleared his throat, warning the intruder he was aware of their presence. He heard a shuffle. However, they didn't come out from wherever they were hiding. "Show yourself," he said gruffly. "Otherwise, I shall fetch the sheriff."

"Oh!" The voice was soft and sounded feminine. Why on earth would a woman be hiding in here? At the inn. And why would she be accompanied by the smell of horse excrement? The entire scenario seemed rather unbelievable.

He took a few steps forward, then stopped as he reached the bed the maid was yet to strip and remake. Charles leaned down and pulled the bedding aside. There, underneath the bed, huddled in a corner was the last thing he expected to see.

"Well," he huffed. "You are not what I expected to find." He held the bedding up out of the way to allow the woman to come out. "Whatever is that dreadful smell?" he asked as she shimmied across the carpet and out from under the bed.

At first glance, he believed the intruder to be young. Only now he could see her in the light, it was clear she was not at all young. She was closer to Charles' age, and he was said to be past his prime.

He reached out and helped the trespasser to her feet. She was unsteady, and he sat her on the side of the bed where he glanced down at her feet. It was then he noticed the manure on his expensive carpet. He was not thrilled at the prospect and knew it would take some time to clean. Room fifteen would be out of action for possibly days.

He glanced angrily at the woman balanced on the edge of the bed. Her face ashen, and her entire body shaking. "What on earth are you doing here?" he demanded gruffly. "This is a blatant case of trespass," he added, to ensure she knew exactly where things stood.

"Please don't call the sheriff," she begged. "He'll put me in jail, and I didn't do anything wrong."

"Huh!" Charles said, unable to hold back his annoyance. "You are trespassing in my inn, plus you've ruined the carpet. I'll have to get a professional in to clean it." He stared down at the woman who was now twisting her hands in her lap. "What are you doing here anyway?" he demanded, his demeanor abrupt. He'd worked hard to build his business up to the level it was at now. Thankfully the inn was not fully booked over the next week, so having one less room would not cause any financial deficit.

Without warning, the woman lifted her chin and stared into his face. "They're trying to kill me," she said quietly, then tried to run. Charles grabbed her by the arms to stop her, assessing the mess spreading further over the carpet as the minutes ticked by.

"You can't just leave without punishment," Charles told the woman, until finally her words sunk in. "What? Who is trying to kill you?" he demanded. More likely than not it was a figment of her imagination. Or even more likely, a story she made up to avoid being charged by the sheriff and thrown in jail.

The woman could be a vagrant. Except when he took the time to look her over, she was well dressed, and apart from the unmistakable odor of the stables, appeared to be far from the beggar he initially thought her to be.

Now Charles was confused. Perhaps what the intruder said was true. He may never know. "What is your name?" he asked, this time more gently. His gruff exterior often landed him in trouble. His temper had gotten the best of him on several occasions.

"Elizabeth Dunagan," she whispered. "But everyone calls me Lizzie."

"Well, Lizzie," Charles asked her, keeping his voice to a low tone to match hers. "What am I going to do with you?"

Chapter Three

Lizzie had no idea how to answer the man's question. He would get the sheriff to lock her up, there was no doubt in her mind.

She also didn't know whether this man merely worked for the innkeeper, or whether he was the owner. He had not introduced himself.

He stared down at her, his expression was one of thought. It seemed he was trying to decide what to do about her. Or perhaps *with* her.

Lizzie didn't blame him.

He was right about one thing – the stench of horse manure was overwhelming in this room. She glanced down at her boots; they were covered in the offending item. "I should remove my boots," she said quietly. "I'm truly sorry for making such a mess of your beautiful carpet." She really was. Lizzie had no wish to damage the inn's property. She merely needed a safe place to hide.

Without warning, he dropped to his knees. "Let me do that," he said, then pulled off one boot, handing it to her before removing the second one.

"What should I do with it?" she asked, her confusion taking over. It was fine to remove them in order not to do further damage, but the smell – the closer to her face it was, the worse it got.

It was all Lizzie could do not to vomit.

As if sensing her discomfort, the man ran into the bathroom, quickly returned with a towel. Placing it on the floor, he then took Lizzie's boots from her. Would she ever see them again? She certainly hoped so. She also wished they would be spotlessly clean when they came back, and didn't have that awful smell.

As if he only now realized he didn't introduce himself, he cleared his throat once more. "I am Charles Lovett," he said gently. "This is my inn."

That told Lizzie her entire future was in this man's hands. It didn't sit well with her, but what choice did she have? Lizzie knew everything that happened to her now would be of his choosing.

"Your clothes…" he said, letting his words trail off.

"The livery is not the cleanest place in town," she told him. "I had nowhere else to hide. Besides, I knew Big John would protect me."

Charles considered her before speaking again. "Big John?" he queried, then shook his head. "Who is this man? Should I contact him on your behalf?"

Lizzie stared at him. Didn't everyone in town know Big John? She thought they did, but going by Charles Lovett's words, he clearly did not. "Big John is a horse. My childhood horse," she said quietly.

"Of course," he said. "Pardon me if my mind is a little befuddled." Not surprising, Lizzie decided. "I'll take your boots and have them cleaned," he told her, not waiting for any further explanation.

Lizzie stood. She didn't want to sit on the edge of the bed any longer. What if she ruined the bedding too? Wherever she went, Lizzie left a trail. A tainted one.

What would happen to her now, Lizzie had no idea.

She felt vulnerable and a shiver went through her. This man, who was quite tall, being the inn owner, he was in a position of power over her.

"Thank you." Lizzie glanced down at her stockinged feet. His eyes followed her gaze. "Once my boots are back, I'll get out of your hair," she said. Where she would go, Lizzie did not know, but she couldn't stay here. She'd already caused Charles Lovett enough trouble.

He squinted and studied her. "Where will you go?" he queried, keeping his voice low. "Or more to the point, who are you running from?"

It was a fair question. She knew it was. Lizzie wasn't certain she wanted to disclose what she'd seen, and the resulting pursuit of their only witness.

~*~

Sitting in Charles Lovett's private quarters, wrapped in a clean, dry blanket was somewhat comforting. He had insisted Lizzie remove her clothing and wrap herself in the thick blanket before they left the room she'd hidden in.

He was nothing but a gentleman and waited outside while she undressed. Taking her belongings from her, Lizzie was instructed to stay exactly where she was until he made certain arrangements.

"I have arranged for clean clothing," he said gently. "It should arrive soon." He studied her. She'd had a hot bath and felt a lot better as a result. It didn't, however, negate the fact she was being pursued by killers. "What can I do to make you more comfortable?" He was certainly trying to help, but Lizzie wasn't sure it was the best thing he could do.

Getting her out of his inn and handing her over to the sheriff would be the safest thing for Charles Lovett and his staff. Her heart thudded. What if they came here looking for her? Lizzie already knew they were cold blooded killers. Only a few of Charles' staff knew she was here. He'd told her so only moments ago. Only those he trusted implicitly knew, and they had been with him from the beginning.

That was all well and good, except if they were murdered by the bank robbers, Lizzie wouldn't be able to live with herself. If they killed her, fine. But these people were trying to help her. They shouldn't lose their lives as a result.

"Do you feel up to telling me what happened?" Charles asked, his voice so soft she could barely hear him speak.

Lizzie opened her mouth to tell him, but a knock at the door interrupted her.

"My apologies." Charles said, then crossed the room to the door and opened it. An older woman stood there holding a tray. He took the tray from her, and before he could stop her, the woman pushed her way inside.

"My dear girl," she said, heading toward Lizzie. "I can't imagine what you've been through." She sat on the arm of the comfortable chair where Lizzie sat wrapped in that protective blanket. "Clean clothes are coming. I've brought you a cup of tea, and some cookies if you feel up to it."

She waved at Charles to pass over the tea. Lizzie wasn't sure how she was meant to handle tea when she was holding tight to the blanket to protect her modesty. She finally found a way to hold onto the blanket with one hand and snake the other hand out of the blanket. The tea had been placed on a small table next to her, and she reached for it. At the same time, she lost her grip on the only thing that protected her from embarrassment. The blanket.

"Oh Lordy," the woman said. "You should go, Mr. Lovett," the older woman said firmly. "And find out what's happened to those clothes."

Charles stared at the woman. His face incredulous. "This is my… Never mind," he said, then left them alone.

The moment they heard the click of the door, the woman breathed a sigh of relief. "Thank goodness for that," she said. "Mr. Lovett is a kind man, but he has no clue. I'm Martha," she said, finally introducing herself. "I'm the cook, but the boss, he always gets me to look after the lost souls that end up here." A slight smile crossed her face. "He pretends to be stern and intimidating, but he's really a big teddy bear. He'll do right by you," she said.

Martha reached across and adjusted the blanket. What would happen next, Lizzie didn't know. She did, however, understand Martha would look out for her. She was like the mother hen, looking out for those who strayed.

Her presence made Lizzie feel more at home. Even though she was in the home of a strange man who had taken her in. What would happen to her now, Lizzie didn't know. Her mind kept going back to the scene in the bank, where the people she'd worked with for a very long time, years in fact, now lay dead on the cold floor of the safe. The memory of that scene haunted Lizzie, its image relentlessly replaying in her mind.

Chapter Four

Once outside his own private quarters, Charles huffed. He would never get used to Martha bossing him around, even though she did it all the time.

The woman had a heart of gold, despite her harsh exterior. He'd seen it many times before. She pretended to be tough as nails, but he knew better. When Bessie arrived at the inn, desperate for work, he'd seen it then, too.

She had already taken over caring for Lizzie, and knew she was in good hands. He would chase up the clothes, but he was almost positive the boots were beyond redemption.

He was on the cusp of finding out what happened to Lizzie when Martha arrived. Perhaps she would get the story from the woman who had disrupted his entire day. Not that he was annoyed. Charles was far more concerned about her safety to be cross about being interrupted.

He headed down the stairs toward the front reception desk. One of the maids had been tasked with purchasing clothes from the mercantile. After all, Charles couldn't go to the mercantile and buy women's clothing. It simply wouldn't be right. Besides, it would get the townsfolk talking.

The gossips came up with enough unsubstantiated stories without him adding to the mix. Which brought him back to the question on hand – what was he to do with this terrified woman who had dared to trespass on his property?

He had to give it to her. Lizzie had ensured her safety by sneaking past him, and possibly other staff members in the light of day. She had already proven herself to be resourceful. It was a character trait he admired.

Charles wandered down to the reception desk. Bessie, the young maid who'd found Lizzie, was tasked with looking after any unexpected guests who may arrive. She had not been trained in this area, so he trusted she was managing. Except when he arrived there, the desk was unmanned. Glancing about, Charles saw no one. Not a maid, not a porter, and definitely no guests.

The early time of the morning was likely the culprit. It would be at least another hour before any guests would arrive. He glanced through the booking sheets. No one was due to arrive today. It was a relief. Despite that, he marked room fifteen as unavailable. He glanced up as the front door opened. Bessie hurried inside. She held a paper bag, and Charles realized this would be the new clothes he'd ordered for his unexpected guest, Lizzie.

How long his guest would be staying was yet to be seen. If he was any judge, he would have no control over it. Martha would dictate to him as she always did. She seemed to have taken a special interest this time; he wasn't sure why. Perhaps because she was being pursued by goodness knew who?

"Thank you, Bessie. I'll take that," he told her, and the maid appeared disappointed. He could only assume she was curious about the owner of the foot she'd seen.

The parcel now in his hands, Charles headed back to his private quarters. Upon reaching the door, he knocked. On his own door. The irony of it did not appease him.

Martha opened the door. "Yes?" she asked abruptly. "Do you have the clothes?" She didn't offer to let him in and had opened the door only a crack.

Charles tried to see inside, but Martha was having none of that. "I don't know what's in the bag, but this is what Bessie gave me." It was clear to Charles he'd already lost control. Whether he'd get to sleep in his own bed tonight was at the back of his mind.

Martha snatched up the parcel. "Go to the kitchen and ask the girls to make Lizzie a cup of tea and something to eat." She closed the door before he had a chance to respond. Martha had worked for him so long she seemed to have forgotten which of them was the boss, and which the employee.

The thought made him chuckle. Martha did Martha. She didn't stand on formality, and she certainly didn't think twice about ordering him about.

Instead of arguing, not that he could since she'd locked him out, he headed down to the kitchen as ordered.

~*~

Charles was becoming impatient.

He'd been locked out of his private quarters for nearly an hour. What could be taking so long? Pacing the floor, he breathed a sigh of relief as the door to his private quarters opened. Martha exited, then closed the door behind her.

"Miss Lizzie is being pursued by bank robbers. They robbed the bank then killed all the staff. Except her," she said. "I have to go and prepare lunch now," she told him abruptly before adding, "You can go in now."

Charles knew he shouldn't be surprised when Martha left unexpectedly. She'd done the job he asked her to do. At least he assumed she had. The fact she instructed him to go inside had Charles assuming Lizzie was dressed and decent.

Except his mind was in a whirl over her words. He was unaware of any bank robbery here in Helena. *The place was becoming unsafe*, he muttered. *Especially if criminals were going about killing people*. Instead of trying to decipher Martha's cryptic words, he would ask Lizzie himself.

He tapped on the door. *His door*. The place he'd been banned from not so long ago. "Lizzie?" he called through the heavy wooden door. Charles wasn't even sure she could hear him.

Hesitating, he tapped once more. This time Lizzie's voice came through clearly. "Come in," she said, her voice wavering. Charles knew this had to be difficult for her. Even without knowing the full story, having bank robbers involved had to be terrifying.

Stepping inside he found her in the sitting room, which was where he left her. Only now she wore the new clothes he'd requested, along with the new boots. Now they knew the boots fit, he would order hers destroyed. The smell would never go away, and they would not be the same again.

"Thank you for your generosity," Lizzie told him. She'd begun to stand but he waved her back down. "You didn't have to…"

"No, I didn't," he interrupted. "It was the least I could do to help you."

She appeared uncomfortable then. "Even after the awful mess I made of the room."

Charles grinned. "Even after that." He sat on the chair opposite her and studied the strange woman in his sitting room. "What's this about a bank robbery?" He never had been one to mince words, but this time he might have gone too far. His guest grimaced as he asked the question.

"Well," she said carefully, "I work for the bank manager. He…" She swallowed hard, and Charles knew she was trying to keep her emotions intact. "He sent me on an errand, and when I got back, a robbery was in progress. I don't know for sure, but it appeared they'd emptied the safe as everything sat on the floor outside the safe. I had just opened the door when they shot all the staff. I ran for my life."

"And that's how you ended up here?" It didn't really explain the horse excrement.

Lizzie took a deep breath and let it out slowly. "I hid in the livery. In Big John's stall."

"Oh," Charles said. "And yet you are still in one piece." The horse was notorious for his bad behavior. Few people could go near him, let alone be in a stall with him.

"He has been branded as uncontrollable. It's not true. Kindness is all he needs. I've been visiting him for a while now. Giving him carrots and apples. Petting him. We get along."

Charles raised his eyebrows. "He protected you."

"He did. When the robbers tried to get into Big John's stall to search for me, he raised up and made a racket. They decided not to risk it."

"Except now they have a witness on the run." Charles stared at her. Lizzie seemed to be holding it all together, but he knew better. The shaking of her hands was the giveaway. He hadn't really given it much thought, but now he had to make a decision. There was no way he could live with himself if he sent this woman, this terrified victim, out on the streets to be pursued and ultimately murdered.

If it happened, as he was sure it would, he would be accountable. Perhaps not to anyone else, but certainly to himself.

"You must stay here," he said gruffly. His words didn't come out the way he'd meant, but he was genuinely concerned for her safety and wellbeing. "Are they aware of who you are? Your name? The fact you worked at the bank?" He barked out the questions, not thinking about how it affected her – until it was too late. They might have assumed she was a bank customer. Or they may not.

"I don't know any of it," she said, her voice quiet. "It's possible."

Charles wasn't sure what the best plan of action was. One thing he was certain about – he would protect Lizzie with his life.

35

Chapter Five

Lizzie hadn't considered the bank robbers may know who she was. Until Charles Lovett presented it as an option.

She was terrified before. Now she was petrified. What if they had been casing the bank, and knew who all the staff were? Lizzie thought about her little cottage on the edge of town. If they knew who she was, her home and belongings may be targeted, too.

When she left for work this morning, Lizzie's life was happy and uncomplicated. Now everything was uncertain, with danger lurking nearby. She was unsure of her next course of action.

Lizzie didn't want to be beholden to Charles Lovett – the stranger who had opened his home to her. Why he felt obligated, she didn't know, but Lizzie was grateful for his help.

"You'll stay?" Charles voice brought her out of her reflections. What choice did she have? Lizzie knew if she left the inn, she would be a sitting duck.

She was only in the bank for mere seconds, but the robbers saw her. They must have heard the door open, and then slam shut. They had nothing to lose – they'd already murdered her colleagues, and now they would have her in their sights.

A small sound left her lips. It was akin to a quiet scream. Not only was her life out of control, so were her reactions. Lizzie was not a screamer, or a crier, but she was on the verge of breaking down.

"Should I call Martha back?" Charles asked gently. He was studying her closely. It was clear to Lizzie he was not used to emotional women, although she wouldn't say she was emotional right now. She was definitely scared, and didn't know what the future held for her.

Lizzie shook her head. She didn't dare speak for fear of her voice breaking. Or tears falling. But she was strong. Lizzie would not let either happen.

Elizabeth Dunagan, she scolded herself silently. *Pull yourself together.*

If she fell apart, where would she be? Lizzie had learned the hard way there was only one person she could rely on. And that was herself.

Despite her rejecting his offer to recall Martha, Charles disappeared out the door. A few minutes passed, and the cook appeared again, this time carrying a cup of tea. It appeared everything could be fixed with tea. And perhaps a cookie as well.

"Charles said you might be up for a nice cup of tea," the older woman said, and handed it over.

"Always," Lizzie said, although it wasn't really what she thought. If Charles believed a hot beverage would fix everything, so be it. Who was she to tell him otherwise?

"He thinks you are upset," Martha continued. She studied Lizzie, then put a hand to her shoulder. "I cannot imagine how difficult this is for you," she said. We've had girls here before who needed help. Some of our maids have been rescued by Charles. Not that he would admit it," she said, rolling her eyes on the last sentence.

"He sounds like a saint," Lizzie said. Except she'd never met a man yet who could be elevated to saint status. Not one. She smiled briefly, and Martha grinned.

"He's the closest thing to a saint I've ever met," Martha told her firmly. Then her face softened. "Charles is quite concerned about you. He's downstairs in his office, working on a plan to keep you safe."

It was news to Lizzie. She'd assumed he'd left in case she dissolved into a puddle of tears. Still,

Martha could be right; she would probably never know the truth.

"Well, drink up. Tea has miraculous powers – it turns the worst day into something far better." Martha had a way of lifting Lizzie's spirits. It was as though she'd done it many times before. If what she said about Charles saving many of the maids, then she had the experience behind her to ensure Lizzie's peace of mind.

Not that Lizzie was in a position to believe anything would ever be right again. Now though, she would accept the offer of clean clothes and plentiful cups of hot tea.

~*~

Lizzie was startled awake when Charles stormed into his private quarters. She'd drifted off to sleep, right there in the sitting room. The fire blazing was partly to blame, she was certain. Boredom was another culprit, Lizzie decided.

She wasn't used to sitting around doing nothing. Even at night in her cottage, she kept busy. When she wasn't cooking, washing, or cleaning, Lizzie kept herself busy knitting. It was a skill her grandmother had taught her as a young child, and one Lizzie had continued to this very day.

Charles stood in the doorway and stared at her. "Apologies," he told her. "I didn't mean to startle you." He ran a hand through his hair, making it stand on end. Lizzie wondered it if was something he did often. She also wondered if anyone told him what his actions did to his appearance.

The very thought of it made her giggle.

Charles frowned. "What's so funny?" he asked, his face serious.

Lizzie continued to giggle. She couldn't help herself. "Your…" She giggled again. "Your hair is standing to attention," she said between her laughter.

At first, he simply stared, then he relaxed a little and joined in the fun. "Is it really?" he asked, clearly amused. He strode across the room to a mirror and stared at his reflection. "I look ridiculous," he said, then tried to restore his hair to its normal style. After a few minutes, he gave up and went into the bathroom located in his private quarters.

Once he returned, Charles sat opposite Lizzie. His expression was again serious. "We need to discuss your situation, and your future," he told her.

Lizzie's heart thudded. Was he preparing to throw her out on the street, despite saying he wouldn't? Charles had said he would protect her at all costs. Except she completely understood. Now he had the full story, it was too much to bear.

She stood, her legs shaky, and her heart pounding. "I understand," she said quietly. "I'll leave now. If you return my own clothes, I'll…"

"What? No!" Charles bellowed. His loud voice frightening her.

Not only was Lizzie scared, but she was also confused. "You don't want me to leave? Or you do?" she asked, her voice barely above a whisper.

Charles stepped toward her and put his hands gently on her shoulders. "I want you to stay – it's far too dangerous for you to leave." He licked his lips before continuing. "I…I have a plan. We must marry," he said nonchalantly. "I've been informed by the ever-knowledgeable Martha, that I cannot have you in my quarters like this. That it would ruin your reputation."

"I, ah." Lizzie didn't know what to say. How to answer. It wasn't like he particularly liked her. Otherwise, he wouldn't make a mess of his hair the way he did. Would he? "Have you ever been married?" she asked, more curious than anything else.

It wasn't as though he had treated her badly, because he had done the absolute opposite. Charles Lovett had done everything he could do to ensure her safety. And for that, Lizzie was grateful. "That is very kind of you," she said, when a response to her question was not forthcoming. "I should leave.

My presence will have put you and your staff in imminent danger."

"Absolutely not," Charles said firmly. At least he didn't bellow this time. He lifted a hand to run through his hair but stopped himself. Was it because she'd laughed at him? Lizzie had no idea, but she did know she needed to laugh when she did. If she hadn't laughed, she would have cried, and then it could have turned to hysteria.

Her entire world had been turned upside down by two men who had no consideration for others – only for their own material gain. Their actions turned her into someone who could no longer make decisions for herself. Despite saying the words, Lizzie knew she wouldn't last long if she left the inn and went out onto the streets of Helena.

If she returned to her cottage, the place that had been her refuge for more years than she cared to remember, who knew what would happen to her. It left her with little choice.

She took a deep breath and silently counted to ten. His eyes trained on her, Lizzie said the words Charles was waiting to hear. "If you're sure?" she asked.

"It's agreed then. I shall arrange for the preacher to come here later today."

Chapter Six

Charles was certain Lizzie would say no. Her grimace at his suggestion confirmed his suspicions.

Except, in the end, she didn't. He had to admit though, Lizzie came across as a woman at the end of her tether. She was frightened, confused, and overwhelmed. There was no doubt in his mind.

They had not discussed the terms of their marriage, and if he had his wits about him, Charles would ask her to sign a prenuptial agreement. If his uncle Jeremy was alive, he would insist on it. Except Charles was very aware Lizzie had agreed to marry him out of desperation. Not for some greedy grab of his property or belongings. And certainly not for love.

As he watched her now, the hopelessness she felt showed through. Lizzie was on the verge of a breakdown; he was certain of it.

"Should I fetch Martha?" he asked, and Lizzie glared at him. It was enough for him to take a step back.

Lizzie didn't answer, didn't say a word. She did, however, shake her head. Then she stood. And stretched. Then yawned.

Of course she would be tired. Most likely exhausted. What a day she'd had. From his point of view, all Charles had endured was one of his maids almost hysterical, followed by him having to confront *the foot* in room fifteen.

Lizzie had dealt with far more. First, she'd watched her colleagues being murdered in cold blood, ran for her life, and hid in a stall at the livery. Then she'd had to find her way to the inn and hide.

He was being a selfish ass. If Mother were still alive, she'd have roared at him like she did when he was a mere boy. And he would have deserved it. "Would you like to lie down for a while?" Charles suggested. She stared at him, not saying a word. He reached out with steadying hands. Dark circles sat under her eyes, and he knew he was right – she was exhausted and needed to rest.

Her hands clasped around his, and Charles felt a shiver go down his spine. Lizzie seemed weak and could barely stand alone. The day's sad events had taken their toll on her. Instead of helping her walk to the guest bedroom, Charles lifted her and carried Lizzie the short distance. Once there, he laid her down, removing her boots. Her eyes closed and she was soon asleep.

Taking a blanket from the closet, he carefully covered her, ensuring he didn't disturb the sleeping woman who would soon become his wife. His fiancée. He stared down at her. Charles knew once they made those vows, his life would change forever.

~*~

Charles dressed in his best suit, while Martha ensured Lizzie was appropriately attired. Although this marriage was one of convenience, who knew how long they would stay together? Or even if Lizzie found the love of her life sometime down the track. If it happened, he would of course let her go.

He had no idea why, but the very thought of Lizzie marrying another man hit him in the heart. Staring at his image in the mirror, Charles straightened his tie. The jacket he wore was pristine. It was also a little small for his expanding frame.

The last time he'd worn this suit was for Uncle Jeremy's funeral. At least today, the recollections of such a sad day would be erased for happier memories.

Charles shook himself mentally. This was not a day to be celebrated. He wasn't in love with Lizzie, nor was she even slightly smitten with him. It could be considered nothing more than a transaction to keep her safe, and to ensure Lizzie's reputation remained intact.

According to Martha, it was the entire purpose of this fraudulent marriage.

A tap on the bedroom door brought him out of his thoughts. "Come," he said abruptly, wondering who would be bothering him minutes before his marriage ceremony was due to begin.

As he continued to fiddle with his tie, Martha's image appeared in the mirror. "Let me," she said impatiently. It was only moments later when he was ready to marry the stranger currently in his guest bedroom. How did she really feel about preparing to wed him? Charles may never know. Everything he was doing was for her safety.

Lizzie agreed to marry him, but he wasn't convinced she truly wanted to go through with it. When the ceremony was over, he would ensure his bride knew he would allow an annulment the moment she was safe to leave the inn.

The very thought of it cut through his heart. Charles had no idea why – he kept his distance from anyone who affected his emotions. After the last time, he vowed to never get close to a woman again.

What was he thinking, agreeing with Martha? Why did he even listen to the blasted woman?

Charles knew the answer – she had been with Uncle Jeremy for as long as Charles could remember. She was like a second mother to Charles. Whenever he'd come to visit, she would look after him, and ensure he was well cared for.

Jeremy, as much as Charles loved him, was not a good uncle. He was sent to the inn every year to spend time with his father's brother. He was convinced neither of his parents realized how eccentric Jeremy was. Or how truly rundown the inn had become under his uncle's care.

He might have owned the inn, but it was his staff who kept it all running like a well-oiled machine. Jeremy spent most of his time at the saloon playing poker. When he wasn't there, he would bring his poker friends to the inn where they would play into the night.

The memory of those days triggered something from deep inside him. His uncle died at the hands of another. Did that mean he was murdered over a game of poker? Charles would probably never know.

He shook the thought away. More than anything else, he needed to concentrate on the task at hand – preparing for his marriage ceremony.

"You did buy a wedding ring, didn't you?" Martha asked him pointedly.

"My goodness," he exclaimed. "I did not." He suddenly felt defeated. "What should I do now?"

Martha rolled her eyes then crossed the floor to a cupboard in the corner. She extracted a small box and opened it. "This was your Aunt Meredith's wedding ring. It's a family heirloom, since it belonged to your grandmother before Jeremy gave it to Meredith.

"And now I am to pass it on to Lizzie?" Was Martha really suggesting he give a treasured heirloom to a total stranger? "What if she decides to leave me down the track?"

Martha scowled. "It is your job to ensure Lizzie is happy. If she leaves, it will be because of your selfish behavior." She almost threw the ring box at him and stormed out of the room.

Was she right? Was he selfish? Charles had to think about it for less than a minute. Until now, he only needed to concern himself with the running of the inn, and his own well-being. Martha took control of the staff. Mostly because he was an oaf, to use Martha's words, who didn't know how to deal with people. Especially those in distress.

His interactions with Bessie when she found Lizzie in room fifteen was a prime example. Charles vowed to do better.

He only hoped he could.

Chapter Seven

Lizzie's hands shook. As did the rest of her body.

Marrying Charles was the easy part. Playing the part of his doting wife was another thing altogether. It wasn't like he was an ogre. The man was easy to take. At least he was if you saw past his gruff exterior.

She too, could be gruff, and today was certainly a good excuse to behave in such a fashion. Except Lizzie didn't blame anyone for her situation except those murdering bank robbers.

"Are you ready?" Martha asked as she entered the guest bedroom. "I do believe Charles is ready. The preacher is waiting in the sitting room."

Her last sentence took Lizzie's breath away. It was suddenly real. Despite the beautiful gown Martha had sent Bessie to purchase from the mercantile, and the boots he'd bought earlier today, she didn't feel ready.

Bessie had spent considerable time fixing Lizzie's hair to make it presentable for a bride. At least it's what she'd been told. She couldn't deny the style suited her perfectly. Today, Lizzie felt like a princess with all the attention she received.

Sometimes princesses were forced to marry, she reflected. Except she wasn't being forced, but it did feel like she had no option. Lizzie's heart pounded as she stepped out into the sitting room. The preacher sat rigid on the chair nearest the fire, and Charles stood nearby. He too, appeared stiff. Did he feel this marriage was being forced on him?

Lizzie truly hoped he didn't.

"Good. You're ready," Charles said impatiently. "Shall we get this over and done with?"

Surprise filled her. Lizzie believed he was voluntarily marrying her. Charles did not appear at all happy, nor did he seem interested in this marriage.

Martha stood beside him and elbowed him in the ribs. She whispered something to him, but it was illegible to Lizzie. He nodded to the older woman, then stepped forward, taking Lizzie's arm.

He led her to the area where they were apparently holding the ceremony. She hadn't understood how truly large the sitting room was. Although it appeared the chairs had been moved to accommodate the procedure.

With the preacher standing in front of them, Martha and Bessie stood behind them. They were apparently to be the witnesses. It made perfect sense since her presence was known only by a few people.

The preacher cleared his throat, then glanced at Lizzie. Her heart pounded and she felt light-headed. She took some deep breaths and steadied herself. Charles squeezed her hand. It was reassuring. "Are you alright?" he whispered, so only Lizzie could hear.

"I will survive," she whispered back, but wondered if her words could make it true.

"Dearly beloved," the preacher began.

In only a few short minutes, they were married.

Lizzie couldn't believe she'd voluntarily married a perfect stranger. Even under such dire circumstances. And even if he did appear to be the right person for her dilemma.

"You may kiss your bride," the preacher added, much to Lizzie's dismay. She hadn't planned on any kind of intimacy with Charles. Even if it was only a kiss.

He gazed down into her face. His eyes seemed to be asking a question, but Lizzie wasn't sure how she felt in that moment. Lizzie did the only thing she felt she could do and nodded briefly. Moments later,

Charles pulled her gently against him. He wrapped her in his arms and kissed her forehead.

It was as if he was saying *I'm here and I'll protect you*. For the first time since she witnessed the murders of her colleagues, Lizzie felt truly safe. How long the feeling would last, she had no idea.

What she did know was she didn't want it to end.

Lizzie sat on the side of the bed. In the master bedroom. She hadn't expected to be carried across the *threshold*, even if that was across the bedroom doorway. It was too dangerous to go outside their private quarters, Charles explained, and this was the only alternative.

She hadn't expected it. After all, this was merely an exercise in keeping her hidden and safe. Nothing more. Nothing less.

Except the way Charles looked at her didn't come across that way. He gazed down into her face as though he was assessing her very soul. As though he understood her, loved her.

Lizzie knew better.

This man she'd married was only trying to protect her. How long it would last, she didn't know. What she did know was once the killers were behind bars, they could seek an annulment. Then they could each get back to their normal lives.

For Lizzie though, life would never be the same again. She had watched her colleagues, her friends, being executed in front of her eyes. If she didn't have her wits about her, Lizzie knew she would have been next.

It could still happen.

If the sheriff was unable to find those men, she was doomed to a life inside the inn. If he did find them, would she be compelled to testify against them? A lump formed in her throat. It was the least she could do for the men she worked with and admired. They had done nothing more than go to work this morning, expecting to do what was required, and return home at the end of the day.

Joseph Thornbury, the bank manager, had a wife and six children. Most of them far too young to help their mother. The teller, Peter Constant, had married his childhood sweetheart only last month. Her heart pounded – Lizzie knew had she returned only minutes earlier, she too, would be lying dead in the bank's safe.

"They're still…" She choked back her emotions. Lizzie glanced up at Charles who appeared to be studying her. Tears swam in her eyes, but Lizzie would not let them fall. She opened her mouth to finish the sentence, but the words wouldn't come.

Her husband sat down beside her. "They're still what, Lizzie?" he asked her gently. Charles held her hands. He was the person she needed in her time of need.

"Mr. Thornbury and Peter. They're lying dead in the bank's safe." Now she'd said it out loud, Lizzie felt somewhat relieved, but it didn't negate the feelings of dread filling her.

Charles' arm slipped around her shoulders. He pulled her close against him. The warmth emanating from him was comforting, but it didn't take away the pain of reality.

"I will ensure they are taken care of," he said quietly. Charles gazed into her face. Her tears fell – Lizzie could no longer hold them back. He lifted a hand and wiped them away. The gesture felt somehow intimate.

A shiver ran through her. Was this how their lives would be until she was safe again? Until those men were captured and punished?

Lizzie had lived alone for many years. Decades, in fact. Once her parents died, she was left alone. Until now, she had never questioned her decision. Having Charles here with her, holding her, caring for her, Lizzie began to question her entire life.

Chapter Eight

Under the cover of darkness, Charles had sent one of his trusted porters to the sheriff's office. It was too dangerous for Lizzie to have one of his workers stroll out in daylight and fetch the sheriff.

The porter knew nothing of Lizzie's situation. Indeed, he had no clue she even existed. The fewer people who knew of her presence, the safer it was for her. Charles had written a note to the sheriff, asking him to come to the inn as a matter of urgency. He'd sealed the envelope to ensure privacy, and to keep Lizzie's situation secret.

He waited nervously in his private quarters. Martha waited downstairs for the sheriff's arrival. Charles refused to leave Lizzie alone. He'd made the decision she would sleep with him, in his bed, but had yet to inform his new bride.

What Lizzie would say about the decision, he didn't know. What he knew emphatically was he couldn't protect her when she was on the other side of his private quarters. The inn was locked up tight at night, but with criminals roaming the streets trying to locate her, anything could happen.

He must be prepared for every scenario.

It was a long time since Charles had carried a firearm. The inn had been his safe haven, especially as a child visiting his favorite aunt and uncle. But now? He knew the inn was no longer safe. Not for Lizzie, and not for his workers. Thankfully they had no guests tonight. They also didn't have bookings over the next few days. Should anyone arrive unexpectedly, Charles would have to turn them away.

He stood in front of the safe. It was hidden behind a painting in his upstairs office. He only knew of its existence because he'd seen his uncle access the safe once. Before each poker game, Jeremy would remove his gun, along with its bullets. "Best place for firearms," he once told Charles. Despite being adamant about it, he understood Jeremy had lost his life due to taking a gun to one too many poker games.

His hands shook as he dialed the combination, and Charles knew exactly why. There was a possibility he might have to shoot a man to protect his wife. He may even have to take a life. Or two. Whatever it took, he would protect Lizzie.

It's what a husband must do. Shield his wife from the harsh realities of life.

It's also what any decent man would do. The loud click alerted Charles the safe had unlocked. He removed both Colts, along with a box of bullets. His holster was also there. They had all sat in the safe for quite some time. Years.

Charles had always felt safe here in Helena, which was the reason he'd locked the firearm and ammunition in the safe to begin with. Better that, than have the gun go off accidentally.

Only now, his inn was no longer safe. Not through any fault of his, or Lizzie's. The fault lay squarely on the shoulders of the killers. Bank robbery was one thing, but to murder those who cooperated, that was another level of evil.

Until those men were found and put behind bars, no one in Helena was safe. Especially not his wife.

There was a tap at the door. Charles had moments earlier closed the safe and put the painting back where it belonged. "It's the sheriff," Martha called through the door.

Charles secured the holster and loaded the Colts into it. He hurried over and opened the door. "Thank you for coming so quickly," he said, and offered the sheriff his hand.

They sat in the sitting room, near the fire. Charles noticed it was burning low and added two logs to keep it going strong. This time of year, it was cold outside. The least he could do was keep the room warm. Now he had a wife to care for, he would be far more vigilant.

Sheriff Terence Dodd was an older man. He'd been sheriff for as long as Charles could remember and had a good reputation. "What's this about?" he asked, getting straight to the point.

"Murder," Charles said firmly. "Bank robbery, too."

Sheriff Dodd's eyes opened in surprise. "Bank robbery and murder? I need far more information," he said, clearly flustered. He opened his notepad and had his pencil at the ready.

"There was a bank robbery here in Helena," Charles began. "The two employees were murdered."

The sheriff glanced up from his note taking. "You mean three employees?"

"Lizzie Dunagan witnessed the murders and ran for her life. She is here – I've given her refuge." Charles knew he had given her far more than a place to hide. He'd given her hope.

Sheriff Dodd scribbled down the information Charles provided. Thankfully he didn't need to talk to Lizzie today. He promised to come back tomorrow. In the meantime, along with his deputy, the sheriff would visit the bank. A job he wouldn't savor.

By the time the sheriff left, Charles felt more confident the bank robbers would be found. The fact the sheriff knew nothing of the robbery bothered Charles. How could no one have known? Surely there were customers who visited the bank during the day. Helena was a bustling town. The inn staff went there at least twice a week to deposit the takings, and often more.

Several businesses in town did the same. The mercantile, the bootmaker, and the diner, to mention only a few. He found it absurd to think no one had been to the bank that day. Otherwise, they surely would have reported what they'd found.

Did no one visit the bank after the robbery? The thought had Charles confused. It made no sense at all.

He was, however, relieved Lizzie had escaped from the clutches of those horrible men. Otherwise, she too, would be lying in a pool of blood, waiting for someone to report her death to the sheriff.

The very thought of it cut right through his heart.

Chapter Nine

Lizzie drifted off to sleep, but the low whisper of nearby voices had awakened her.

Her husband's voice she recognized, but the other voice was not familiar. It could be the sheriff, since Charles had sent word for him to visit. That was before she'd fallen asleep. It wasn't what Lizzie wanted – she preferred to stay awake and alert.

It could mean the difference between life and death. Not only for her, but also for Charles, and even his staff. Every time the possibility entered her mind, Lizzie felt ill. Her stomach churned at the mere thought of anything happening to these wonderful people.

They had taken care of her, and ensured she was well hidden. All that said, Lizzie knew she couldn't stay out of sight forever. Like other people, she needed to be outside in the fresh air. On the streets talking to people and working. Although Lizzie admitted to herself, she would never step foot in the bank again. Not ever.

The memory of what happened was ingrained in her mind, and she was certain it would be that way for as long as she lived.

If the robbers had their way, her life would be cut short.

Lizzie staggered out to the sitting room. Her clothes were crumpled after falling asleep on the bed. She was convinced she would be forgiven for her disheveled state. Charles turned to face her moments after he closed the door. She didn't ask the question, only stared at him.

"Sheriff Dodd has just left," Charles told her. "He didn't want to disturb you. Tomorrow he'll be back to take a statement. In the meantime…" The words trailing off told Lizzie what she needed to know.

"In the meantime?" Lizzie's heart thudded. Had no one been to the bank? Were the bodies of her dear friends still laying in the safe? The vision of them being shot sprang into her mind again. The murders took only seconds, but the memory would last a lifetime.

"Lizzie," Charles whispered as he led her to the chair nearest the fire. "My dear, Lizzie." Her name on his lips sounded special. Important. She allowed herself to be seated. "Sheriff Dodd and his deputy are headed to the bank. There has been no report of a robbery. Or anything else."

Lizzie shook her head. How could that be? There must have been at least one customer there today. Surely. The thought of her dear friends still lying dead on the cold floor of the bank's safe broke her heart. "Does that mean…?" She couldn't finish the sentence. The words simply would not come.

Charles reached for her hands. "Sheriff Dodd will take care of everything," he said gently. "No need to upset yourself."

Lizzie glared at him. Did he think she would simply forget about the people she had worked with for several years? Or their families? Heartache hit her all over again. Pushing her feelings aside was not working. Would not work. Instead, Lizzie let her tears fall. She was not an emotional woman, never had been. This was all too much.

Within a period of less than twelve hours she had witnessed not one, but two murders, fled to save her life, not once but twice, then married a complete stranger in order to keep safe and protect her reputation.

How she would move forward from that, Lizzie had no idea.

~*~

The knock at the door startled Lizzie. She had fallen asleep in the big comfortable chair next to the fire.

Charles kept the fire burning constantly, which meant the room was always toasty warm. It was the way she liked it. The memory of the bitter cold, as she ran for her life sent a shiver down Lizzie's spine. She had been chilled to the bone but continued to run. She had no choice.

If she hadn't, she would now be lying dead somewhere. Likely in a place no one would find her. At least for days.

An involuntary sob left her lips. Charles rushed over to her, and wrapped Lizzie in his arms. "What is it?" he asked quietly. Behind him, Martha placed their meals on the large mahogany dining table. The aroma of food permeated the room, but Lizzie wasn't at all hungry.

"Memories," she whispered. "I don't think they'll ever go away."

Charles gazed into her face. He didn't say anything, but it was clear he agreed. "Martha has made a lovely meal for us," he told her. "Do you feel like eating?"

She didn't want to offend Martha, but wasn't convinced she could stomach anything. Instead, she nodded. "I can try," she said. Even if she only had tea, it was better than nothing. Wasn't it?

When she glanced across the room, Martha was gone. She had cared for Lizzie as though she was

Martha's own daughter, and for that, Lizzie was grateful. These people, these strangers, who until today, didn't know she existed, had saved her life and probably her sanity.

Charles helped her to her feet, and Lizzie took a step, then stumbled. Ever vigilant, her new husband was there to ensure she didn't fall. He was a man of honor, and his strength had gotten her through the tragedy she had witnessed. She didn't know how long it would last, but for now, Charles was her rock.

As if sensing her fragility, he lifted her and carried Lizzie to the table. He gently sat her down, then seated himself next to her. Next, he poured tea for her. Lizzie reached out. Tea was what she needed right now. Except her hands were shaking.

Would she never feel normal again? His strong hands covered hers, and he brought the cup to her lips. Lizzie stared at him over the edge of the warm liquid. His eyes were filled with compassion. He was there for her, and Lizzie was thankful.

Except she knew it couldn't last. He'd only married her because he'd been pushed into a corner. Once this madness was all over, he would instigate an annulment. She was certain of it. A man of his age, one who had never married before, had to be set in his ways. If he'd truly wanted to marry, he would have already done so.

No matter how comfortable she felt with him by her side, how protected he made her feel, Lizzie knew this marriage would only last however long it took to find the men who were determined to kill her.

Chapter Ten

Charles was fussing, he knew he was. He was concerned about Lizzie's welfare. She'd barely eaten all day and had consumed mostly tea. It wasn't enough to sustain her. Not short term, and certainly not long term.

Perhaps tomorrow he should get the doctor to check her over. Except the fewer people who knew she was here, the better. Her safety was paramount. His hands now covering hers, Charles wondered how long it would take for the shaking to stop.

She'd had a terrifying shock, there was no doubt in his mind. Those men, those murderers, they did this to her. Once they were behind bars, she would begin to heal. Charles knew in his heart Lizzie likely would not ever completely get over what she'd witnessed today. Nor would she heal from the fear of being pursued by men who were determined to eliminate her.

His heart shattered. He may not have known Lizzie for long, but he felt every emotion she displayed, as well as those she held inside. He couldn't completely relate – of course he couldn't. Charles had never been in her shoes, but for the grace of God.

He helped Lizzie bring the empty teacup back to the table and let her simply sit and contemplate her next move.

Martha was such a blessing. She'd made thick vegetable soup, accompanied by freshly made rolls. If Lizzie ate nothing else, this food would sustain her until morning. The trick would be to get her to eat.

He'd already resigned himself to the fact Lizzie was unlikely to contemplate, let alone eat, the roast chicken meal. Tasty as it sounded, with an aroma that quickly drew him in. He pulled the covering off the soup and placed it in front of Lizzie. She leaned closer and breathed in the fragrant aroma.

"It smells delicious," she whispered, but made no attempt to eat it. She did, however, reach for a roll. He pulled the butter closer and watched as she lavished the roll with it. Did that mean she would eat something after all?

Charles watched her closely, then averted his eyes. Was his close observation disturbing to her? He wondered why he hadn't realized it before. "I…I need to check the fire," he said, using it as an excuse to leave her alone for a few minutes. Would it be long enough for Lizzie to eat? His examination of her every move had been polarizing. He was now certain of it. "You'll be alright?" he asked. When she nodded, he cautiously left her side.

In the sitting room, he went over to the fire. It was burning nicely, as he knew it would be. He fiddled with the logs in the firebox, to give the pretense of actually doing something. Charles did not like deception, but convinced himself this was the only way to put Lizzie at ease. Hopefully when he returned, she had eaten something. Anything.

After what felt like enough time to get the fire sorted, he returned to the dining room. Lizzie was exactly where he'd left her. It appeared she hadn't moved, not even an inch. As he got closer, Charles could see she'd eaten part of the bread roll. He was more relieved than he thought possible. Had she touched the soup? Sitting down beside her, he could see she'd at least attempted the soup. She'd eaten almost half of what Martha had given her. Warmth filled him. At least now he didn't have to worry about her going hungry.

She glanced up. "I can't eat any more," she said quietly. "Is it alright if I go back to the sitting room? Or I can stay here with you," she added, her last words uncertain.

It was now clear to Charles the sitting room was where she felt most comfortable. Was it the large cozy chairs? Or the roaring fire? He suspected it was a combination of both. It was his favorite room, too. Charles spent many evenings simply sitting in there, contemplating life. He was fully aware he lived a privileged life. Martha reminded him of it often.

Still, until today, he hadn't realized how very true it was. From his observations, Charles concluded Lizzie was not poor, but she wasn't rich either. She deserved better, and he would ensure her life was easier from now on. "You go," he said firmly. "I'll be along shortly. Or do you need my assistance?" He was a fool. Of course she needed his help. Instead of waiting for an answer, Charles stood and helped Lizzie to her feet.

Once he'd settled her in the sitting room, he was reluctant to leave her alone. No matter what he told himself, Charles' heart was already governing his every move.

He reluctantly left his wife alone, even though she seemed more settled now. Almost the moment she sat on the chair, the one nearest the fire, she seemed more relaxed. She rested her head against the back and closed her eyes. Lizzie was sound asleep before he even left the room.

Before he returned to the sitting room, he covered her with a blanket. In sleep, Lizzie appeared far more relaxed than he'd seen all day. He knew, despite the chair being comfortable, it wasn't made to sleep in. If he left Lizzie there all night, she would be stiff and sore in the morning.

Apart from the fact he was meant to be protecting her. He couldn't do so if she slept in one room, and he was asleep in yet another room. Charles rolled his shoulders. His neck and shoulders were tight and stiff. It wasn't at all surprising. Today had been a nightmare.

If it had been so bad for him, what was it like for Lizzie? He couldn't even begin to imagine the horrors she had witnessed. Or the terror of being pursued by the men who robbed the bank and brutally killed her colleagues.

Reluctantly, he began to walk away. To leave Lizzie alone, to let her sleep in peace. She began to mumble in her sleep. Before long she was crying. Her weeping turned to sobs. What should he do? The consensus was to never awake a sleeping person in the midst of a nightmare. Or was that when they were sleepwalking?

Now he couldn't remember and didn't know what to do. Charles had never been so confused in his life. Instead of battling with himself, he went back to Lizzie and wrapped her in his arms. He would provide whatever comfort possible. Even if she was not aware, it seemed to be helping.

He stayed with his arms around the sleeping woman for what seemed hours. Finally, she settled. Instead of leaving her there to awaken to stiff limbs and an aching neck and back, Charles carried her into the bedroom. He pushed back the covers and lay her gently on the bed. Lizzie's boots presented a problem, but he finally removed them without waking her.

Once he'd pulled the covers over her, he returned to the dining room. He was no longer hungry, but Charles had to listen to his own advice and eat something. The food was barely warm, but he ate the soup, and some of the chicken.

Ensuring the door to his private quarters was locked, Charles returned to the bedroom where Lizzie lay sound asleep. He wasn't sure how well he would sleep tonight. Not only because he wasn't used to sharing his bed.

He patted his hip. The Colts were still there and were fully loaded. As he undressed, he slipped one gun under his pillow and climbed in next to his wife.

The next few days could be interesting. If not downright dangerous.

Chapter Eleven

When Lizzie awoke, a slither of light shone through the window coverings. How she'd slept this long, she wasn't sure. One thing she did know, she hadn't taken herself to bed, which meant Charles had carried her there.

He was a good man, her husband. It would be a sad day when they applied for their annulment, but it was inevitable. No matter how long it took, Lizzie knew Charles would be there for her until those killers were found and jailed.

So many thoughts ran through her mind. The main one had plagued her since the moment she'd walked into the bank. Why did those men kill the bank manager and teller? They had what they wanted — there was money, gold, and expensive jewelry stored in the safe. Why didn't they simply leave once those items were in their possession?

Several bags of their loot sat on the floor, outside the safe. Peter was a mere teller. He had no authority to open the safe. Nor did he know the combination. Mr. Thornbury, as the bank manager, was the only person with that information. Why then, was he murdered once he'd given the robbers access to the safe?

The question bothered Lizzie more than it should. Her boss had never been anything but kind. He was a husband, and father to six children. Now his wife was a widow, and his children fatherless. A simple robbery had turned to murder. Why? The outcome was more than Lizzie could fathom.

Bank robberies occurred on a regular basis. Few turned to murder. Her heart hammered, and Lizzie felt ill. Her racing thoughts churned her stomach, and she was going to vomit. She suddenly sat up and ran to the bathroom where she emptied her stomach of the small amount of food she'd eaten the day before.

"Lizzie?" Charles voice carried through the door. "Are you alright? Should I come in?"

The thought of Charles seeing her like this made her feel worse. "Don't come in!" she shouted. "I'll be alright in a minute."

He was silent. Did that mean he'd gone away, or was he listening, waiting to know if she truly was alright?

Lizzie went to the basin and let the cold water run over her hands. She splashed the water on her face and rinsed her mouth. She glanced in the mirror, but it was too dark to truly see her reflection.

Still, she stared at herself, no matter her image was almost nonexistent in the darkness of the room. "What is your future?" she asked her reflection. "Do you even have one?"

"Lizzie!" Charles called urgently. "Who are you talking too?" She could hear the dread in his voice.

Lizzie opened the door. "I'm alone," she said quietly. "I was giving myself a stern talking to." He stared at her. "It didn't work," she said, tears now streaming down her face.

Charles pulled her close and held Lizzie tight. "I will always be here for you, Lizzie. I promise."

Being held like this, Charles made her feel loved and protected. Except Lizzie knew their marriage was only temporary. It would last only until the killers were jailed, or until they found her, and ensured she couldn't testify against them.

Charles attended to the fire while Lizzie sat in what had become her chair. The constantly roaring fire in the sitting room always seemed to warm her. Not only in body, but in mind. A feeling of peace always came over her when she sat in this chair. It was the very reason she gravitated to this particular spot each time.

She glanced across at Charles. He was staring at her, a smile on his face. "You look so peaceful sitting there," he said quietly as he began to stand.

"I feel that way, too," she answered. "This room is always warm and cozy. It gives me a feeling of calmness and makes me feel as though everything will be alright." She gazed at him, wondering what Charles was thinking. "It will be, won't it?" she asked urgently. Lizzie couldn't bear to think her being here would put others in danger.

He reached for a blanket and placed it across her lap. "Everything will be alright," he told her gently. "I promise." His last words were more forceful than Lizzie expected.

She studied him before responding. "You can't promise something so important, so..." She fought for the right word. "...life changing." Lizzie knew she was right. By the expression on his face, Charles also knew it was a promise he shouldn't have made.

"You're right," he said as he came to stand beside her. "I will do my very best to keep you safe." There was nothing more she could ask of him.

Lizzie craved tea. Her stomach was still in turmoil, and she was not prepared to eat, but tea would help settle things. At least she hoped it would. A knock at the door startled her. Charles put a hand to her shoulder. "It's alright," he said. "Martha is bringing breakfast."

Instead of being comforted, the thought of food had her stomach churning all over again, but Lizzie was determined not to let herself vomit again.

On opening the door, Lizzie heard a man's voice, which she wasn't expecting. She stayed right where Charles had left her. If he wanted her to move, he would come and tell her.

A short time later, he returned to the sitting room, accompanied by another man, Sheriff Terence Dodd. Lizzie knew who he was but had not met him personally. She'd seen him at the bank on rare occasions, as well as wandering Helena on his rounds. He was responsible for keeping the town safe, she knew that much.

When the pair stared down at her, their expressions filled with sadness, Lizzie knew what was to come. "I'm afraid the news is bad," Sheriff Dodd said. "Mr. Thornbury and Peter Constant are both dead."

Lizzie swallowed hard at the news. She expected confirmation her work colleagues were dead, but it didn't make the news any easier to bear.

Charles motioned for the sheriff to sit down. He sat on the edge of Lizzie's chair and held her hand. It was a relief for Lizzie. She didn't like the pair towering over her.

"We also found someone we believe to be a bank customer in the safe," the sheriff continued. His words were slow, meant to ensure every word sunk in. "We are yet to identify him, and I wondered…"

"No," Charles said firmly. "My wife is not leaving the inn until it is safe to do so."

Sheriff Dodd gazed at Charles. "I would never ask that of Mrs. Lovett," he said coldly. "I only wondered if she knew if Mr. Thornbury had any appointments yesterday. It might help us identify the third victim." His face softened, and Lizzie instinctively knew he was trying his best to protect her from the harsh realities of what had occurred.

Lizzie was confused. "There were no scheduled appointments this week. Could it be a customer?" Unexpectedly, Lizzie's eyes filled with tears. Not only for the unknown victim, but for her work colleagues and their families.

Charles squeezed her hand, then leaned down and gently kissed her forehead.

"Thank you, Mrs. Lovett. I didn't recognize the man. Perhaps he was from out of town." Sheriff Dodd said, then turned to walk away.

"Did…" Lizzie needed to know. "Did you find the men who did this?" she asked quietly. Before he even answered, Lizzie knew the answer. They were still out there somewhere. Wandering around Helena looking for their one and only witness.

"I'm afraid not," the sheriff told her, then let himself out of the private quarters where Lizzie felt safe. But for how much longer?

Chapter Twelve

Charles watched Lizzie closely. She didn't flinch at the sheriff's words, nor did she cry. Although tears swam in her eyes. He was certain she would be thinking about her co-worker's families, along with the unknown victim. Everyone in town knew the bank staff. They were the heart of the town and were loved by all who met them.

She felt especially sorry for the as yet unknown victim. He was simply in the wrong place at the wrong time. Had he arrived a little earlier or later, he would still be alive. On the other hand, being sent to do an errand for her boss saved Lizzie's life.

When he studied her, Charles could almost read her mind. Victim guilt was real, and Charles was certain it was what Lizzie would be experiencing right now.

"I was at the mercantile, talking to Mae. Mrs. Ridgeway," Lizzie said, her voice breaking. "I had no idea the bank was being robbed. My colleagues…" She stopped abruptly and swallowed. "I'm only alive because I was at the mercantile doing errands?" Her eyes already filled with tears;

Lizzie was no longer strong enough to force them back.

Charles squatted on the floor next to her. "None of this is your fault. The only people to blame are the killers. The men who robbed the bank are to blame. Not you, not the bank manager or teller, and certainly not the stranger whose life was taken from him."

Lizzie shook her head. She didn't believe a word he'd said to her. It wasn't surprising. It was quite common for people in her situation to feel this way. Charles reached out and pulled Lizzie to her feet. He enveloped her in his arms and held her close. "None of this is your fault," he whispered.

She may not believe him, but Charles would do whatever he could to persuade Lizzie.

He flinched at the knock on the door. This time it would be Martha. Tea was what Lizzie needed, and it would be part of Martha's delivery for breakfast. "I have to let Martha in," he said, glancing down at the upset woman. He helped her to sit down again, then opened the door.

"Good morning," Martha said brightly. It only took moments for her to realize it perhaps wasn't as good as she first believed. In whispered tones, Charles explained the latest information.

"Oh my, the poor girl," she said, hurrying past Charles. She left the tray on the table, and swooped up the tea, taking it to Lizzie.

Lizzie's head shot up as Martha entered the sitting room. "I've brought you tea," Martha told her. Charles worried his cook might bring up the situation at the bank, but she didn't say anything about it. He should have known better – Martha was the height of discretion when it was required.

"I heard you have an upset stomach," she said. "This will help." Without another word, she poured tea from the pot into the dainty cup covered in delicate red roses. She added a small amount of milk, then handed it to Lizzie on an equally delicate saucer.

Lizzie glanced up and smiled. "Thank you," she said quietly. "I appreciate your efforts. And I feel a little better now." Her smile was forced, Charles could tell, but he totally understood why she felt this way. Her entire life was in turmoil. She was in danger and her friends murdered. To top it off, Charles knew for certain Lizzie felt guilty for not being one of the victims of the bank massacre.

He had a lot of work to do if he wanted to have any hope of making Lizzie feel anything like normal ever again. The only way he knew to do that was to keep her safe and smother her with love and kindness.

Even then, it may not work. If that happened, Charles wasn't sure what he would do.

"I've left breakfast in the dining room," Martha said. "If it's too much, I can make something lighter."

Charles knew what Lizzie would say before she even opened her mouth. "My stomach is still a little churned. I will enjoy this cup of tea though," she said wearily. "Thank you, Martha."

Martha hesitated, then put a hand to Lizzie's shoulder. "If you change your mind, Charles can let me know." She stared at him then, daring her boss to challenge her.

"Of course," he said. Anything for Lizzie. She may not have been here long, but he already had feelings for her. Whether it was because of her situation, or for a completely different reason, he wasn't sure. Only time would tell.

Martha began the short trek out of his private quarters. "If you need anything, come down and let me know," she said as Charles opened the door.

Charles held back a chuckle. When he was a small boy visiting his uncle, Martha looked out for him. She also bossed him about. He might be older now, no longer a child, but so was Martha. He respected his elders, and although Martha wasn't elderly, she wasn't young either. He would never disrespect the woman who ensured he was well-fed and cared for during his childhood visits.

He was thankful for Martha's continued presence at the inn. She looked out for the younger women, and ensured his belly was always full. She didn't hold back when it came to criticizing his actions either.

This time the thought yielded a chuckle. Thankfully, Martha had left, and the heavy wooden door closed. If she'd heard him laugh, Martha would have words with him about his lack of respect. It was a speech he'd heard many times as a youngster. She did, however, ensure his attitude changed, and quickly too.

The inn's cook was like a second mother to him.

Charles shook himself. He didn't have time to dilly-dally. His wife, the thought made him pause. Yes, she was his wife, even if in name only, and he had to ensure her safety and peace of mind. Only right now, he knew she was far from either of those.

He lifted the lid on the breakfasts Martha had made. As usual, she'd made a huge breakfast for him — bacon, eggs, sausages and tomato. Not to mention the copious pieces of toast she always sent.

The second plate contained less, and a much lighter meal. Scrambled eggs with bacon and two slices of toast. It was as though the cook was psychic. Except

Charles knew it was more likely she understood the needs of women.

He reached for the mug of coffee and took a mouthful. As though it sustained him, Charles went back to the sitting room where he'd left Lizzie. She was basking in the warmth of the fire. He'd hoped by now she might have calmed down, but her face was still taut, and her eyes glazed. Charles believed the flames of the fire may have contributed to that but couldn't be certain.

"I'm back," he said gently, not wanting to startle her. "Did you enjoy your tea? Martha made a light breakfast for you, if you feel up to it?" He took another mouthful of the coffee, hoping it would help him feel more relaxed. It didn't.

She glanced across at him. "The tea was good. Martha is a kind soul," she said. "I…I'm not sure I can eat anything," she told him, her eyes suddenly sad.

Charles would not try to force her. He would never do that. "Should I call the doctor?" he asked gently. Although he was certain he already knew the answer.

Lizzie shook her head. "I'm sure I'll be fine," she said, then turned away to stare into the fire.

Charles stood. He needed to eat, even if Lizzie was not interested. "Will you excuse me for a few minutes?" he asked.

"Of course," Lizzie told him. She turned back to face him, then pulled the blanket up around herself.

Charles studied her for long moments. She surely couldn't be cold. Lizzie sat right next to the fire. Puzzled, he continued to study her.

Finally, it hit him. Lizzie was in shock. Getting the doctor was the best option, but the fewer people who knew about her existence, the better. Instead, for now, he would monitor her condition himself.

Chapter Thirteen

Lizzie snuggled under the blanket Charles gave her. The fire was roaring, and the room was warm. In reality, she didn't need the thick wool blanket, but huddling under it helped keep her calm.

Nothing would happen to her, Lizzie was certain. Charles would keep her safe. Still, the knowledge of her assured safety didn't appease her. She simply couldn't get the vision of the murders out of her mind.

There was a tap at the door. She heard Charles speak quietly. Was it Martha or one of the kitchen staff come to take the breakfast tray? If it wasn't, who was it? Charles didn't let just anyone come up here. The area was blocked off from the rest of the inn. It truly was private.

A shiver ran down her spine.

Lizzie was told when she was first brought to Charles' private quarters, they had come through a private entrance. It had made her feel secure. Except she didn't remember any of it. Now she worried about being attacked here despite reassurances from Charles.

Keep calm, she told herself to no avail.

"Martha brought a pot of tea for you," her husband told Lizzie quietly. Despite the muted sound of his voice, she was startled. He stared at her. "I'm sorry. I didn't mean…"

Shaking her head, Lizzie responded. "It's alright. You didn't scare me." Except Lizzie knew it was a lie. He had frightened her. To the extent she was on the verge of running. Where to, she had no idea.

Charles carried a small tray with the tea, a mug of coffee, and an assortment of cookies. He placed the tray on a side table, then poured the welcome beverage and handed it to her. "Martha is very thoughtful," Lizzie said. She sipped at the hot tea, as her eyes glanced over the enticing cookies offered to her. "Not for me," she told Charles. He frowned.

"You haven't eaten anything today," he said gently. "Please try at least one." The worried look on his face left her guilt-ridden.

Lizzie nodded and reached for one of the delicate offerings. "Thank you," she whispered, still unsure if her stomach would react badly. The cookies had been lovingly made, she was certain. Martha seemed to put a part of herself into everything she did. "They're delicious," she said, after taking a bite. She quickly finished it and sipped her tea once more.

Almost immediately, Charles pushed the tray of cookies toward her again. "Another?"

She stared up at him. Her husband was determined to have her eat something. Even if it was something as indulgent as cookies. Lizzie supposed she couldn't blame him. After all, men were meant to look out for their wives.

Still, this was new for both of them. Neither had been married before. At least it was what Charles had said when asked by the preacher. She had to assume he wouldn't lie about such a thing. Especially to a preacher.

Lizzie shook herself mentally. Charles Lovett was not the sort of person to bend the truth. Not even a little. She glanced up at him, only to see he was still studying her. Still waiting for an answer about the cookies. Her guilt pushed her over the edge, and Lizzie reached for a second cookie. A different one this time.

"I haven't seen *you* eat," Lizzie said firmly, holding the cookie mid-air.

Charles straightened. "I," he said gruffly, "ate breakfast." Despite his words, he reached for one of the small cookies.

Lizzie only could imagine the clockwork of his brain churning. He popped the cookie in his mouth, all at once, no less. The vision made Lizzie giggle. This big man popping a teensy cookie in his mouth. It was funny. Even if Charles did not see the joke.

"What's so funny?" he asked, his voice a little abrupt. He frowned momentarily, still having no understanding of her reaction.

His words somber, it immediately stopped Lizzie in her tracks. Instead of answering, she studied him. He reached for a second cookie and popped it in his mouth. Nothing changed. It was still funny. This time, instead of giggling, she laughed out loud.

Charles' hands flew into the air. He shook his head and glanced down at the plate of small cookies. Then a smile crept across his face. He finally got it. "Is it really that funny?" he asked, chuckling between the words.

It was the relief they both needed. A good laugh despite the dire circumstances. It would do them both good. "You had to see it from my point of view," Lizzie said, then laughed again.

Charles finally sat down. He didn't look so big, so overpowering when he was at her level. He reached for the mug of coffee and sipped. His face softened. She could get used to this, Lizzie decided. Sitting next to the fire like she was the Lady of the Manor and Charles her Lord.

They may not live in a mansion, but this apartment was as close to one she'd ever been. They sat in silence, each silently studying the other as they enjoyed their hot beverages. Strangely enough, the awkwardness silence often brought was no longer there. This silence was comfortable; neither felt compelled to speak.

The moment his mug was empty, Charles stood. "I'm afraid I have work to do," he announced, then headed to the dining room.

A shudder wracked Lizzie's body. Was he leaving her alone? Her entire body went stiff. What if someone broke in and attacked her? Bracing herself, Lizzie tried to relax. She struggled to convince herself he would still be on the premises. Knowing it was the case, she should be fine.

"I'll be in my office," he added, then opened a door she hadn't even noticed. There was a room behind the comfortable chair she sat in. Lizzie had not explored the apartment; her mind was elsewhere.

Now she knew Charles would be nearby, she could relax. At least for now. But now she was curious. Lizzie only waited long enough for Charles to enter the room, then stood. She wanted to know everything about the man she'd married.

What he liked, including food, what didn't sit well with him, and his work ethics. Charles sat behind the large mahogany desk, pen in his hand, papers in front of him. She slowly entered the room, not wanting to startle him.

Although Lizzie was certain he wasn't a man to be easily scared. His head shot up as she stood in front of his desk.

Charles placed the pen on the desk. "To what do I owe the pleasure?" he asked, a smile on his face. She had never seen Charles angry and wondered if he ever lost his temper. In her estimation, it would have to be something quite serious for it to happen.

"Curiosity," she said, running a finger along the edge of the desk. Lizzie expected to find dust, but none was there.

He waved a hand toward the chair that sat opposite his own. "Take a seat," he said, his words more formal than Lizzie expected. Did he bring important guests up here? Surely not. Although it would be decidedly more private.

She glanced about. The room was luxuriously furnished. Apart from the large, expensive looking desk, two lounge chairs sat on the other side of the room, along with a small side table. A large painting hung on the wall. When he glanced up, Charles could study it. Lizzie wondered if he ever did.

Perhaps it was there to hide a safe? She would probably never know. "How often do you work in here?" She wanted to know as much about him as she could determine. As her husband, it's what she needed to do.

As her temporary protector, getting to know him was probably the worst idea she'd had for a very long time.

Chapter Fourteen

Charles hated the fact he needed to work.

He wanted to spend more time with Lizzie but having her in his office was a distraction he didn't need. They may not have known each other for long, but he already had feelings for her. His unexpected wife was unlike anything he'd anticipated.

What he did expect, Charles wasn't sure.

Of course, being pursued by killers would have a major effect on anyone. As much as she was kind, and caring, he wasn't convinced he was seeing the real Lizzie. It wasn't surprising. He acknowledged it had to be challenging for her.

Not only could she not go to her own home, but Lizzie was also without her belongings, her clothes, and everything she held dear. It broke his heart to even think about it.

"I adore this room." Lizzie leaned forward in the chair, then continued to glance about the room. Her eyes seemed to land on the painting more often than he expected. Then she smiled coyly. "Is there a safe behind it?" She squirmed in the chair, as though it was a question she shouldn't have asked. Lizzie waved a hand in front of herself. "Forget I asked," she said, then leaned back in the chair.

Charles raised his eyebrows. It was like a scene out of live theatre. The thought made him smile. Despite the situation, despite the odds, she still managed to make him smile. Warmth filled him.

A loud knock at the door startled them both. Charles frowned. He pulled out his pocket watch and checked the time. "Stay here," he said firmly. He closed the door behind him, leaving Lizzie to wait inside.

He opened the door carefully, leaving only a small gap. He breathed a sigh of relief on seeing Sheriff Dodd standing there. His deputy was standing nearby. Charles first thought was the news couldn't be good.

"Charles," Sheriff Dodd said, his voice solemn. "The bodies have been removed, and the bank is now locked up and out of bounds."

"And the killers?" He already knew the answer before the sheriff told him.

His deputy answered, his tone one of compassion. "In the wind," the deputy said. "But I believe they are still in town."

This couldn't be good.

Charles opened the door wide to let the two lawmen inside. Both men glanced about. They were clearly looking for Lizzie. "My wife is in my office. I will fetch her, but please be discreet with your information. Understandably, she is rather fragile." He indicated for them to sit on the chairs opposite Lizzie's favorite chair.

The two men glanced at each other then sat. "Understandably," the sheriff said.

Opening the office door, Charles went inside. "The sheriff and his deputy are here." He kept his voice as normal as possible. What he wasn't expecting was the look of dismay on Lizzie's face. He went to her side and pulled his wife to her feet. "It's alright," he told her, then pulled Lizzie up against him, and wrapped her in his arms.

Charles knew he shouldn't be doing this, but it was clear she needed reassurance. "There is an update of the situation. I'll understand if you don't want to know." He continued to hold her in his arms, and warmth flooded his entire body. Lizzie leaned her head against his chest and her body seemed to sag.

Did that mean she was relaxed around him now, or was she relieved in anticipation of getting the latest information? He would probably never know. She glanced up at him, and briefly nodded. "I'm ready," she said, then added, "At least I think I am."

Charles patted her back. It was meant as an endearing assurance he would be nearby. She looked more confused than relieved. Instead of explaining, Charles let his arms slip to his sides and urged her into the sitting room.

The moment Lizzie was out of the office, she stopped in her tracks. She stared across at the two lawmen waiting for her to join them. They both stood. "Mrs. Lovett," Sheriff Dodd said.

His words were echoed by the deputy.

Lizzie sat in what had become her regular chair – by the fire, where she felt comforted. She didn't speak but waited for one of the lawmen to bring her up to date.

Sheriff Dodd spoke, after clearing his throat. "We have…er, cleared the bank and locked it up tight. I don't expect you'll want to go there again at any point?" He didn't give Lizzie time to answer and continued his narration. "I've been interviewing some of the townsfolk. Two men…" He glanced across at Charles before continuing. "It appears two strangers have been asking about their *missing sister*. Trying to locate her."

Charles heard her gasp at the sheriff's words. He put a hand to Lizzie's shoulder. "They're still here," she whispered, her voice cracking.

Sheriff Dodd ignored her statement. "Tell me what the bank robbers look like."

Lizzie stared at him. "First, I want more information from you. Where were they asking? Who did they ask, and what information do they have about me?"

For a minute, Charles was speechless. His meek and mild wife had found her voice. He wanted to applaud her, but decided it was inappropriate given the situation.

The sheriff licked his lips before speaking. "They described a middle-aged woman with wavy brown hair. The story they gave was farcical. Their *sister* was off her head, they said, and needed constant care. At least that's what they're saying." He ran a hand through his hair. "I don't believe they know anything about you, Mrs. Lovett. They certainly don't have much of a description. They don't even know your name."

Lizzie frowned. "They don't? What are they telling people?"

This time the deputy spoke. "When asked, they changed the subject. It was the case with every person they spoke with."

Lizzie sagged with relief. "They have no idea who I am," she said, tears swimming in her eyes. Charles felt every bit as relieved as his wife. He wanted the sheriff and his deputy to leave so he could hold Lizzie as she absorbed this new information.

"I expect they will eventually make their way to the inn," the deputy told them. "I assume your staff can handle it when it happens?" He studied Charles, challenging him to say no.

"I will make arrangements. There will be someone behind the desk who can handle it, even if that person turns out to be me."

Lizzie stared at him, then. "You…you can't," she almost wailed. "You've already risked your life for me." This time tears rolled down her cheeks.

"It is time for us to go," Sheriff Dodd told them. "Thank you, Mrs. Lovett. I'm sorry the news wasn't better." Charles saw them both out and hurried back to Lizzie.

"Please don't do this," she said, her voice breaking.

Charles held up a hand to stop her protests. "If someone is to be harmed, it won't be any of my staff. I'll work something out," he said firmly, then took Lizzie in his arms and held her close.

Chapter Fifteen

Lizzie's heart was breaking. This wasn't what she wanted. She hadn't come to the inn to hide, only to put those who worked here in jeopardy. It was now clear she hadn't thought her actions through before hiding here.

Her heart pounded, but Lizzie knew what she needed to do. "I will work on the front desk." She heard Charles' gasp but ignored him. "When the killers come asking about me, I'll give myself up."

Charles rolled his shoulders. The stern look on his face told Lizzie she needed to stop talking. Except she didn't. "If anyone is going to be harmed, it will be me." She stared at him, daring Charles to protest.

He closed his eyes, but only for a moment, then shook his head. He gazed into her eyes as though trying to fathom her motive. To Lizzie, it was perfectly clear – she'd put people in danger, and this was the best way to remove them from it.

Charles opened his mouth to speak, and Lizzie was certain he would bellow. Except he didn't. His voice was soft, gentle. "None of that is happening," he told her. "I am your husband, and the role of husbands is to protect their wives." He reached out an arm and pulled her close. "I will protect you, Lizzie. Under no circumstances, will you go downstairs. Do you understand?" he asked, his voice still low.

"But…"

Charles glared at her. "No buts," he said, this time much louder. More forceful. Then he pulled her close and wrapped her in his arms. "There will be no more discussion on this subject," he added, and Lizzie's heart shattered. It meant he would allow others to take the risk. Or…he would take it himself.

Lizzie hated this. Hated the fact, through no fault of her own, she had inadvertently put innocent people in danger. The worst of it was she had no way to fix this – short of running away.

Her husband was keeping an eye on her, ensuring she was safe at all times. For Lizzie, it meant she had little hope of getting away. If she so much as mentioned any of this to Charles, she didn't know what he would do.

To be truthful, she did. He would ensure she couldn't leave – for her own safety.

She already felt like a prisoner up here, behind locked doors. Even if she did get away, where would she go? It was a question she had asked herself many times. If she went back home, to her little cottage at the edge of town, would she be safe?

It seemed very clear, at least to Lizzie, the killers did not know who she was. Not her name, nor the fact she worked at the bank. Perhaps if she managed to get out, she could go home. The trick would be disguising herself, so she wasn't seen by those despicable men. Lizzie was certain they knew what she looked like. Except the sheriff hadn't mentioned it.

She leaned into Charles, and simply enjoyed the moment. His heart beat strong against her ear. Lizzie felt contented when he held her. Although she certainly wasn't happy at that moment.

He leaned closer to her. "Don't even think about leaving," he whispered, and her head shot up.

Her eyes burned into his. How did he know she was thinking along those lines? "How did you…?"

"We may not have known each other long, but already, I know you too well," he said firmly. "I need to think on this," he said, then kissed her forehead, sending shivers down Lizzie's spine. "I have one goal, and one goal only – to keep you safe when I cannot be near."

Lizzie sighed. What was Charles planning? She wouldn't know until it happened. Of that, she was certain. Especially when he knew she would object if it put other people at risk. Vehemently object, as she would.

~*~

There was so little for Lizzie to do during her *confinement*. Soaking in a hot bath was most enjoyable, and she savored every moment of it. Charles said he would use the time to tackle the paperwork that awaited him.

She lay back in the bath and let the heat soak into her skin. Lizzie was enjoying the luxury of Charles' home, even if there was a dangerous element to her being here. She could easily live like this for the rest of her life.

Except Lizzie knew it wasn't an option. Besides, to stay married, she needed to be in love. She was far from those feelings. Sure, she felt comfortable with Charles. His arms holding her gave Lizzie a sense of contentment, but none of those things meant she was in love.

Besides, he had no feelings for her. Instead, Charles Lovett had anointed himself as Lizzie's protector. He was the sort of man who, if he made a promise, kept it. He was certainly keeping to his end of the bargain.

Lizzie had nothing to offer in exchange. She slid further down into the water. It was so peaceful here, and the water was relaxing her. So much so, Lizzie felt ready for a nap. Except it was the middle of the day.

Without warning, she was on alert. She heard a click; was it the front door closing? Did it mean she was now alone? Lizzie swallowed back her panic. Charles wouldn't leave Lizzie on her own, she was confident.

He had been pedantic about ensuring he was with her the entire time. Why would he choose this moment to leave? Because she was occupied with her bath? Did Charles think she wouldn't notice he was gone?

She glanced at her hands. Lizzie's skin had begun to pucker. The water had cooled down to lukewarm. It was time to get out of the bath. Except Lizzie knew the real reason was to ensure she hadn't been left alone.

Her heart thudded. Could she take this opportunity to leave? Did she even want to do so? Something told her she needed to discard the idea altogether, and simply enjoy her luxurious surroundings while she could.

Lizzie stayed in the bathtub despite the chilly water, then pulled the plug. She watched the water circle like a miniature tornado until all the water was gone. All the time her mind was ticking over, wondering what was occurring outside the bathroom door.

She reached for the fluffy white towel Charles had left for her. Everything he did for her, big or small, seemed to come from a place of love. Lizzie shook the thought away. Not only was it ridiculous, but it was laughable. How could Charles, a man she had only met days ago, be in love with her? The truth was, he couldn't be. It was as simple as that.

With the towel now draped around her shoulders, voices drifted through the apartment to her ears. Voices, not one voice, but at least two. Had the sheriff returned? And if so, was the news even worse than last time?

Chapter Sixteen

Charles heard the bathroom door open, then close again. Dagnammit. He'd hoped Lizzie would stay in the bath longer.

He glanced down at his watch. His biggest regret was making the decision at the last minute. Now she was about to confront him about what he had done. It couldn't be taken back, and even if it could, he wouldn't do it.

It was for her own safety. He had to keep telling himself that, especially when Lizzie objected. As he knew she would.

Lizzie confronted Charles, hands on hips, before he could attempt to hide his actions. Did he even want to hide it? Before long, everything would be in full swing. There was no going back, so she might as well hear the truth.

"What are you doing?" she demanded, her eyes falling to the Colts in the other men's holsters.

As if he realized what was happening, right before his eyes, Phillip Woodrow spoke. "Mrs. Lovett," he said gently, "we are here to protect you. Phillip Woodrow," he said, offering his hand, but Lizzie hesitated. "This is my associate, Mack Sherman." Charles could see she was conflicted. She was trying to decide if she should accept this man's hand. If he was trustworthy.

"Phillip and his team come highly recommended," Charles said firmly. "We're fortunate to have them."

Lizzie glared at her husband, her damp hair dripping down her clothes. Even when she was angry, Lizzie was still the most beautiful woman he had ever set eyes on. "We need help with this situation," Charles told her. "*I* need help," he corrected himself. "I cannot ensure your safety twenty-four hours a day. Phillip and Mack are one half of the team. You will have around the clock protection."

The flabbergasted expression now on Lizzie's face put Charles on alert. Then she glared at him again. It may have boded well to tell her in advance, but knowing his wife, she would have, no doubt, tried to talk him out of it.

Her eyes went from Charles to Phillip, then to Mack. The pounding on the door startled her.

"I'll get it," Phillip said firmly. He'd been secured by Charles less than an hour ago and was already reassuring him of Lizzie's safety in his hands. As he strode to the door, Lizzie's eyes followed his every move.

The moment Phillip opened the door, Martha pushed her way inside. "They were here!" she announced, her voice in a panic. "Those men, they were here, asking about Lizzie." Martha shuddered as she let out her pent-up breath.

Phillip waved for Mack to check it out. He locked the door behind his associate then followed Martha inside. Thank goodness Charles had the forethought to introduce them earlier.

His arm went around Lizzie, who Charles knew would be in a panic. Heck, his own heart was pounding, so he could only imagine how Lizzie was feeling.

"Slow down, Martha," Phillip said calmly. "Tell me exactly what happened."

Charles guided Martha into a chair. Her face was ashen, and she was clearly in distress. "Two men…they came into the inn. Before I'd even had a chance to welcome them, they asked about their *sister*. She was missing they said, then described Lizzie almost perfectly." Tears filled Martha's eyes. "I didn't give you away, Lizzie, I promise."

"I know," Lizzie said gently, clearly concerned for her new friend.

Martha glanced up at the man hired to keep Lizzie safe. "I told them we haven't had any guests check in for several days, which is true. I'm not sure they believed me."

The tap on the door alerted them Mack had arrived back. "There's no one around," he explained, once inside.

"Can you describe the men, Martha?" Phillip's voice was gentle, almost fatherly. He pulled out a notebook and began writing.

Martha stared at him momentarily, then closed her eyes as though trying to picture each man. "The tall one, he was about Charles' height. He had short black hair, and a scar on his face."

Phillip's head shot up, and he glanced at Mack. "Where was the scar?" he asked, keeping his voice gentle.

Despite that, Charles heard the excitement in his voice. At first it confused Charles, then he realized the pair knew who they were dealing with. At least they thought they did.

"The scar went from his ear, all the way across to his nose," Martha said. "It was fully healed; the scar wasn't new."

"And the other man," Phillip wanted to know. "Can you describe him?"

"Shorter," Martha said. "But not too short. He was only slightly shorter than the other man. He had black hair, too. But his was far longer. It reached his shoulders and was unruly. It looked like he hadn't washed it for weeks, maybe months." She shuddered again. "They looked similar, but this one didn't have a scar."

"You did very well, Martha. Thank you for your help."

Charles studied the two security men he'd hired. They glanced at each other several times while Martha described the inn's visitors. He was convinced they knew who they were dealing with.

"I'll go downstairs in case they return," Charles said. "I don't want them going off uninvited searching the rooms."

"Agreed," Mack said. "That would not be a good idea."

Charles opened the door and was shadowed by Mack. As much as Charles was glad for the company, he was certain he could handle this alone.

~*~

Charles wished he'd brought his paperwork down with him. He'd sat behind the reception desk for over an hour, and nothing had happened. Nothing of any significance, anyway. He left Mack to look after the desk, knowing they would not have any guests while he was gone.

Entering the kitchen, he asked Bessie to make two mugs of coffee and bring them to the front desk. He also requested tea for the two women, and coffee for Phillip.

Bessie didn't question him, but immediately began to prepare the beverages. Martha had trained the girl well. She would include cookies or cake with each tray. It suited him fine, and he was certain Mack and Phillip would appreciate it too.

"Do you think they know she is here?" he asked Mack when he returned to the reception desk. Charles was eager to know if his wife was in imminent danger.

Mack studied him closely. Trying to no doubt gauge if he could handle the truth. "To be honest, because I believe you would prefer the truth, I don't think they have a clue where she is."

Charles nodded, feeling quite relieved. "Is that because they've been asking at all the businesses?"

"It is exactly the reason," Mack replied. "Besides, if they thought she was here, knowing those two, they would have forced Martha to take them to each and every room."

Now Charles was fearful. Not for himself but for his staff. "I don't know what to say to that," he said, his voice low and shaky.

Mack put a hand to Charles' shoulder. "You did the right thing getting us to help. Those two are notorious. They have been known to kill anyone in their way."

A shiver went down Charles' spine. By all accounts, Martha had been lucky. He would not put her, or any of his staff in such a dangerous situation again.

Chapter Seventeen

Martha still appeared distraught by the experience with the two killers. She couldn't be certain who those men were, but Phillip and Mack seemed convinced it was them.

Lizzie reached for Martha's hands and held them tight. "I'm so very sorry, Martha," she said gently. "You should not have been in this position. If I hadn't come here…"

Martha interrupted. "It's not your fault. The blame lies solely on those murdering thieves." She was already ashen, and now she was ghostly white.

Phillip moved from the doorway and sat opposite the two women instead. "Martha is correct," he said. "Neither of you are to blame. Those killers have a lot to answer for." He ran a hand through his hair. It seemed to Lizzie he was trying to make a decision of some importance. "Those two are part of a gang. The marshals have been chasing them for a while now." Phillip frowned. "It's strange only the two of them are here." He rubbed his hand across his chin, but didn't elaborate.

Lizzie wondered if there were more gang members to come out of the woodwork. It sent a shiver down her spine. "There's more of them?" she asked quietly. There was no bravado when it came to killers. She was scared and didn't care who knew it.

"It could only be the two men here in Helena," Phillip told her. "Or the others could be planning other robberies. With more than one bank in Helena, it is highly possible."

Lizzie wasn't sure she could take any more bad news. Her heart thudded and she squeezed Martha's hands. The two women huddled close together. When she glanced at Phillip, it seemed he regretted providing the information. He swore under his breath, which confirmed Lizzie's suspicions.

"You need to talk to the sheriff and his deputy," Lizzie said urgently.

Phillip shook his head. "I cannot leave you ladies alone. When Mack and Charles return, I will go to the sheriff's office."

His words gave Lizzie some reassurance, but there was still the possibility of the two murderers coming after her here. "I can use a gun," Lizzie told him. "It's been a while, but I know what I'm doing." Now her security appeared shocked. "I was raised on a farm. Learning to handle firearms, and how to shoot was mandatory."

She didn't elaborate – didn't feel the need to do so. Phillip was only here for a short time, and Lizzie had no intention of telling him more about her life than even Charles knew. It wouldn't be right.

Without warning, the sound of a key turning in the door had Lizzie on alert. Her heart pounded.

It was then a terrible thought stuck her. Were Charles and Mack still alive? Tears began to fill her eyes. *Had the two men been murdered?*

Despite her terror, as the door began to open, Lizzie's eyes trained toward its direction. Except she couldn't see it from where she sat. She quickly stood, then began to carefully step toward the sound. Phillip called her back, but Lizzie refused to comply. If anyone was going to die today, it would be her.

As she hurried toward the sound, she heard footsteps behind her. Phillip was right behind her.

Lizzie had never been so relieved in her life as when she heard Charles' voice.

"It's only me, Charles," her husband's voice called. Looking back, she saw the stupidity of her actions. Worst case scenario – it is what was going through her mind. Instead of being positive, her mind went to the absolute worst outcome.

At first, she couldn't understand why, but as Charles held and comforted her, Lizzie began to comprehend. Despite the brief time since she arrived at the inn, she had already become more than a little attached to Charles.

This entire scenario was playing with her mind. She glanced up and Charles smiled briefly. He was trying to console her, that much was clear.

"Anything of importance happening downstairs?" Phillip asked. Mack was clearly still there, which begged the question as to why Charles came up alone.

"Nothing at all," Charles told her security detail. "I did have an idea though. What if I put a sign on the door to the inn to say we had unexpected damage, and needed to close for a few days?"

Lizzie's legs felt weak. If Charles hadn't been holding her up, she was convinced she would collapse. "No, you mustn't do it," Lizzie protested. "I will not allow you to lose money because of me."

Charles stared at her momentarily, then glanced at Phillip. His expression clearly said *help me*. Only this wasn't Phillip's choice. Nor was it Charles'. Lizzie could not allow her husband's business to suffer because of her.

Phillip cleared his throat, then spoke. "It's a good idea," he said. "This way, we can check every room and ensure no one is hiding out in any of them. My other two men will arrive tonight, and then we can do a thorough check."

Lizzie's heart began to race, and she felt lightheaded. The thought those killers could be hiding somewhere here, in the place she believed was safe, terrified her. Lizzie was far more concerned about everyone else, than herself. She did not want to put others at risk, and now it appeared to be exactly what she'd done.

Charles stared down at her. She was clutching his suit jacket, trying to hold herself up. An arm slipped beneath her and he carried Lizzie back into the sitting room, placing her on the chair nearest the fire. The heat was comforting, and Lizzie leaned back in the chair.

Charles sat nearby, which she found comforting. "I know you are concerned about my business," he told her. "There are no bookings for several days, and it's rare to have guests who have not let us know they are coming."

"It's true," Martha said. "If we had guests coming, I'd be working in the kitchen instead of sitting on my backside in here. Which reminds me," she announced to anyone who cared to listen. "I need to prepare for supper. After all, these men need their food." She stood and hurried toward the door.

Charles's arms dropped and he stepped toward the door. "I'll come with you," he said.

It seemed to Lizzie she increasingly relied on Charles. It was not what she wanted to do. As soon as this was over, they would go their separate ways. Neither one spoke. As much as she protested over Charles' decision to temporarily close the inn, she simply didn't have the energy.

Everything was happening far too quickly.

First the murders, then the threat on her life, not to mention the speedy marriage. It all happened before she even realized what was going on. She was in shock when she agreed to marry Charles, but he was a good man. How could she complain about that?

Except in time, when her world was back the way it should be, their marriage would be annulled. Then Charles would be alone in his private quarters again, and Lizzie would go back to her lonely cottage on the edge of town.

It didn't bear thinking about.

Chapter Eighteen

Charles walked with Martha down the stairs. Not because she was in any danger, but he didn't want her to feel as though he was putting her in danger.

He accompanied her all the way to the kitchen, then followed her in. Glancing about, he noticed the only assistance she had was Bessie, one of his maids. "Where is everyone else?" he asked without thinking. Most of the staff were only part-time. They were scheduled to work only when the inn had guests, except Bessie who cleaned rooms after their guests had left, then helped in the kitchen the rest of the time.

Apart from all this kerfuffle going on at the moment, it would normally only be himself, Martha, and Bessie. The other staff were not due to work again until next week when a number of guests were due to arrive.

What it meant was they only had a matter of days to catch those men, or he would have to turn his paying guests away. Most of whom were repeat customers.

Charles shook himself mentally. It was all such a mess. It was not anyone's fault, especially not Lizzie's so he wasn't looking to blame. And wasn't it his idea to close the inn? He still believed it was the best option given the circumstances.

If the doors were closed and locked, the killers could not enter his establishment. "We have two more security men coming later," he told Martha. "I don't know what time they will arrive."

Martha acknowledged his words with a nod of her head. "I know, but thank you for the reminder," she said. "Now please, get out of my kitchen and let me work." She grinned, then reached for an apron.

Charles chuckled. Martha never minced words. She said exactly what she meant, and Charles appreciated it.

After leaving the kitchen, he headed toward the inn's entrance. He locked both the large doors, then went behind the counter to prepare a sign. He wrote in big black letters.

The inn is temporarily closed due to unexpected but urgent repairs, he wrote. Then he added, *Apologies for the inconvenience.*

He read and reread the notice, then attached it to the inside of one of the glass panels. As he fastened the notice, he stared out the window. Two men were on the other side of the street, pacing along the boardwalk. Now and then, they glanced in the direction of the inn. "I think it's them," he told Mack. "On the opposite side of the road."

Mack suddenly stood and joined Charles at the door. He studied the men, and Charles could see the concentration on his face. He recalled the descriptions Martha had provided, and was even more sure these were the murderers. The taller man had short black hair. He was too far away to tell if he had a scar or not. The second man was short, but his unruly black hair reached his shoulders, just as Martha had described.

Locking the doors had been timely as far as Charles was concerned. "What time are your colleagues arriving?" he asked Mack.

"I believe it will be around supper time," the other man commented.

It wasn't as though it would make a difference. Martha had allowed for them, so they would be fed no matter what time they arrived. They were capable of protecting Lizzie, which was the main thing Charles cared about.

His precious Lizzie. He had grown increasingly enamored with her as the days rolled by. He had never before truly been in love, but with Lizzie, it had hit him like a ton of bricks lying on his chest.

He wondered if Lizzie felt the same but rejected the idea the moment it entered his mind. Watching the men on the other side of the road, Charles became ever more concerned. The tall one reached into his jacket and pulled out a gun. "You saw that, right?" he asked the other man.

"I did," Mack responded. "There's little we can do until they try to get in here."

It was then a thought hit him. "If that is definitely those men, we at least know they are not in the building."

Mack agreed.

It wasn't much later before Martha arrived with coffee and cake. Her heart was in the right place, but Charles knew if he kept eating like this, he would start to put on weight. Lizzie on the other hand, she was ghastly thin. "Thank you, Martha, but you didn't have to," Charles told her.

"Well, I appreciate it," Mack added. "I am rarely spoiled the way Charles is." He chuckled then, and Martha grinned.

"I aim to please," she told him.

"Martha," Charles said, coaxing her over to the door. "Are these the men who came looking for Lizzie?"

Martha gasped. "It certainly is," she said, her voice shaky. "Oh! Is that a gun?" She hurried back into her kitchen without waiting for an answer.

Charles didn't blame her. It wasn't safe standing near the door, he decided, and joined Mack behind the reception desk.

They sat behind the desk for the next hour. Charles was certain there was something more productive he could be doing. Paperwork could wait – it was not what he meant. Was there a way to catch the two men stalking his inn, and effectively Lizzie?

According to Mack, it was not possible. He was on alert at the knock on the door. Charles heart thudded. Until he realized the killers would not knock.

Mack stood. "It's my two colleagues," he announced.

Charles locked the door behind the pair and moved them to a safer spot – behind the reception desk. Mack introduced Charles to the newcomers and prepared to take them upstairs. It was then bullets began to rain over the front of the inn.

Chapter Nineteen

Lizzie sat impatiently, waiting for Charles to return. Not only was her boredom overwhelming, but she was nervous. Or more accurately, worried.

Phillip sat opposite her but said nothing. Did nothing. He was like a statue, barely moving.

Until he wasn't.

Phillip stood and hurried to the door, put his ear to it. He cautiously opened it and listened carefully. He closed it again, locked it. He still said nothing.

Lizzie's heart pounded. What was going on? "What…what is it?" she asked, fearful of what he'd heard.

Phillip studied her. His eyes silently observing. "I'm not certain," he finally said, his voice even. As though he had not a care in the world.

Now Lizzie was annoyed. "Yes, you do," she said forcefully. "And if you don't tell me, I'm going to find out for myself." Her legs felt weak, but she would do exactly what she'd said if he didn't tell her the truth.

He suddenly clutched her arm. "I'm sorry, Lizzie, but you can't leave." She stared at his hands restraining her, then glared at him. "It's far too dangerous," he added.

Now she was furious. "Tell me right now," she ground out. First, he wouldn't give her a gun, then he refuses to update her, and now Phillip held her, stopping Lizzie from leaving.

Phillip studied her. "I believe I heard gunfire," he said resignedly.

Her eyes opened wide. "I have to go down there now," she said, far more forcefully this time.

"Not a chance." Phillip kept his voice steady, but firm. At the same time, he maintained his grip on her arm. "My other two men should be here by now, which means there are four of them defending the inn."

Lizzie understood his reasoning, she really did. Only she could not allow anyone to die defending her. *She* was the problem, not those four innocent men downstairs. Their deaths would be on her conscious for the rest of her life.

All she wanted was to go downstairs and offer herself up. Let them kill her and let the others leave unharmed.

"I know what you are thinking," Phillip said gently. "Believe me, most of the people we have protected have been the same." He led her back to the sitting room, ensured she sat comfortably, then sat down opposite her. "They all want to put themselves in harm's way to shield those defending them."

Lizzie gasped. Her jaw dropped, and she shook her head. "But…it's no one's fault but mine."

"Did you rob the bank?" Phillip demanded. His eyes bore into Lizzie's. "And kill those people?" He paused, letting his words sink in. "Because unless you did those things, you are not to blame. Not in any way, shape or form."

Lizzie knew what Phillip said was true, but still couldn't accept it. "If I hadn't come here…" she began.

"If you hadn't come here to get away, you would be dead by now. There is no getting away from it." His hands dropped away, no longer restraining her. He now seemed convinced Lizzie would be compliant.

As much as guilt still consumed her, Phillip had made his case. He had convinced Lizzie she wasn't to blame for all this…whatever it was…going on around them. She acknowledged she was safer here, upstairs away from the gunfight and the killers, but what if all four of those men were dead?

What if the killers found Martha and Bessie? They would not let them live; she knew it in her heart. Tears filled her eyes. They returned to the sitting room, and Lizzie took her place in her favorite chair. She faced the fire, not allowing Phillip to witness her weakness. No matter what she faced, how guilty she felt, or who was murdered protecting her, Lizzie needed to be strong.

For the others.

~*~

Lizzie jumped to her feet as she heard the key turning in the door.

"Stay!" Phillip bellowed, and for once, she didn't move. Despite that, Lizzie was on alert, and her entire body quivered.

Then she heard voices but couldn't make out who was talking. It was more like a murmur to her ears. How many voices she was not sure. The killers could be right there at the door, guns held to Phillip's head.

Lizzie was ready. Ready to die. She should have let them kill her at the bank. Making the decision back then would have meant avoiding all this bloodshed and murder of innocent people.

She couldn't stop the tears flowing down her cheeks. A sob left her lips. Not for herself, but for the loss of Charles, her husband, even if their marriage was only a pretense. Lizzie admitted to herself she was in love with Charles. He was the sort of man she would have fallen in love with under different circumstances.

Not because he had money – it didn't factor at all. He was strong when she was weak. He was protective and caring, and comforted her when she needed it.

A hand touched her shoulder, and Lizzie gingerly opened her fingers. She expected to see a gun pointing at her head, instead Charles hovered over her. Not a scratch on him, as far as she could tell. She sobbed again.

Charles pulled Lizzie to her feet. "It's over," he whispered, then held her tight. The killers are dead. They hadn't figured on the manpower we had. Four against two." He leaned in and kissed her forehead.

Lizzie wanted to relax into him, but her body was stiff. She was terrified of what might have happened. Now it was all over, and she could go home.

Except Lizzie didn't want to leave here.

Not ever.

~*~

The aftermath of the shoot-out was like a whirlwind.

The sheriff and his deputy had seen the whole thing and fired the kill shots. At least it was what they were saying. Less paperwork that way, Sheriff Dodd had said. No one seemed to care – the killers were dead, and Lizzie no longer feared for her life.

Over the course of the last week since the bank robbery, her life had changed dramatically. Working at the bank, Lizzie felt fulfilled. Assisting Mr. Thornbury had meant something. It helped the community, too.

Now, though, she never wanted to step foot in the bank ever again. The image of the murders still haunted her. Every time she closed her eyes, it played out.

Sheriff Dodd wanted Lizzie to identify the killers. It was the last thing she wanted to do, but knew it had to be done. Charles held her hand, squeezing it to assure her he was by her side.

As they approached the entrance to the inn, Lizzie was shocked by what she saw. The glass was shattered. Walls had been damaged, and the killers lay dead outside the entrance to the inn. Blood poured out onto the boardwalk.

She turned her face away, and Charles comforted her. "It will only take a minute," he said gently. "Once you confirm if these are the men you saw at the bank, it's over. We can put it in the past."

We can put it in the past? What did Charles mean? Once this mess was cleared up, he would surely apply for an annulment. Get it finished quickly – it was her preference too.

Lizzie glanced up at him. Silently questioning his words.

Sheriff Dodd's voice broke into her thoughts. "Well, is it them?" he asked, his impatience clear. As though the sheriff finally realized the two dead men were face down, he kicked at them and rolled them over.

Lizzie stared down at them. "I will never forget the killer's faces," she said. "When they saw me at the bank, it was clear they wanted to kill me too." She swiped at a stray tear, then glanced up at Charles. "It's definitely them," she said firmly. Then she turned to the sheriff. "I'm glad they're dead. I don't have to be afraid anymore. Now I can go home to my little cottage." The last sentence was only slightly above a whisper. Lizzie's heart was shattered, despite knowing this day was coming.

She felt Charles shift next to her. "What if I don't want you to go, Lizzie? What then?"

His words filled her heart with joy. Except Charles hadn't said her loved her. Perhaps he'd merely become accustomed to having her with him.

It wasn't enough.

Sheriff Dodd's words cut into her thoughts. They sounded harsh, even to Lizzie. "Good, now I can get these murdering dogs off my streets and bury them. Good riddance, I say."

Lizzie couldn't agree more.

130

Chapter Twenty

When Charles said those words, Lizzie's head shot up. She stared at him for long moments, and it felt like his heart would stop.

Did she really want to go back to her empty cottage? Despite all the recent chaos, Charles' feelings toward Lizzie had grown. Each and every day he felt more enamored with her.

Whenever he held her, Charles wanted more. He wanted to touch her soft skin, and he wanted to run his thumb along her lips. Of course, as her husband, he had every right to do so. As a decent man who had only married Lizzie for her safety and her reputation, he had absolutely no rights.

Instead of answering, she stared up into his face. Her tongue came out and licked her lips. Charles wanted so badly to kiss those lips. Not out here, though. Not with everyone surrounding them. Watching them.

And certainly not with two dead bodies lying on the ground close by. He still had hold of Lizzie's hand. He gently squeezed it. "We should go inside," he said. We must talk, a little voice in his head told him.

Lizzie nodded.

She glanced about as they headed back to his private quarters. On the way they passed Martha and Bessie. The pair appeared bewildered. Shocked.

Still, he continued up the stairs and took Lizzie to his home. *Their* home. As Charles opened the door, it hit him – he'd never called it his home until Lizzie arrived on the scene. She was the one who made it feel like home. Even in the shocked and battered state she had arrived in, Lizzie still made the impossible possible.

For the first time since he moved into the private quarters after his uncle died, it felt like a real home. A place for him to sit down and relax, even if that was only for a handful of minutes. As he ascended the stairs, all these thoughts came to him.

At first Charles did not want to believe it, but now he was convinced. With Lizzie in his life, despite the dire circumstances, he had purpose. Instead of an empty shell with a number of mostly unused rooms, his *private quarters* had been transported into a home.

No more would he skirt around the facts. He had been lonely all this time. He'd not looked for love, and didn't expect to find it with Lizzie.

He pushed the door open, then swooped her up into his arms. "What are you doing?" she asked, amusement clear in her voice.

Charles grinned. "Carrying my bride across the threshold of our home," Charles said as he stared down into her beautiful brown eyes. He was sorely tempted to kiss those lips but held out.

He wanted to be sure it was what Lizzie wanted. After stepping inside, he placed her on the floor but held onto her. "I love you, Lizzie. I do not want you to leave."

Charles waited patiently for her to answer. If he tried to push her into a quick response, she might turn tail and run.

He watched as she swallowed. Lizzie lifted a hand and caressed his cheek. "I love you too. I don't want an annulment, and I don't want to go home." She leaned in and held him tight. "This is my home. At least it feels that way," she whispered.

If he hadn't been holding Lizzie in his arms already, Charles would have pulled her against him. Instead, he lifted her chin, so she was facing him. He watched as she licked her lips.

This time he didn't hesitate. Charles leaned down and kissed the woman he had come to love with all of his heart.

~*~

Four months later…

Everyone sat around the enormous dining table. Their guests included Phillip and Mack. The other two men who'd put their lives on the line for her, had protection duties elsewhere. Martha and Bessie, who prepared the meals, were now seated at the table, at Charles' request.

Things had settled down since that terrible night. The reception area had been thoroughly cleaned, removing all the glass fragments. The doors and windows had been replaced, and the reception desk had been restored to its former glory.

The inn had been closed for a short time but was quickly up and running again. Room fifteen was only used when they were at capacity – Bessie still didn't like going in there. Charles didn't blame her; she'd been given quite a fright that day. He'd since employed two other maids, leaving Bessie to work in the kitchen permanently.

It was the right thing to do.

Initially Charles referred to it as *that terrible day*. Now, he no longer did. Lizzie making her way here had been a blessing. It had changed his life and outlook for the better.

"I propose a toast," Charles said as he lifted his glass. "To friends and lovers," he said, then chuckled as the color weaved its way up Lizzie's face.

She glared at him.

"We have an announcement," Charles said, his eyes meeting Lizzie's. Murmurs drifted across the table. Martha grinned; Bessie appeared bewildered. "We are expecting a child," he said, his voice portraying the emotion he felt.

He reached over and placed his free hand on Lizzie's belly. "To my wife," he said. "My beautiful and amazing wife."

Epilogue

Two years later...

Oliver Sebastian sat on his father's knee. "Horsie," he demanded.

At his wife's request. Charles converted the large piece of land standing empty behind the inn. He'd ensured there was no way for guests to enter the one-acre lot. Charles would do anything for his family, and this was a relatively easy wish to grant.

Lizzie's request was specific. She wanted a large barn that backed onto a corral. That way she could bring Big John here. The horse had been part of her father's ranch, she'd told him. When her brother, Henry, had sold the ranch after their father's death, the new owners did not want the so-called aggressive animal on their land.

It broke Lizzie's heart to see him locked up at the livery. It soon became clear Big John loved Lizzie. She spoiled him with apples and carrots, and when it was possible, she rode him.

While he was locked up, Big John wanted nothing more than to be free to roam at his pleasure as he used to do. He'd had more than enough time in the restraints of the stall. She'd tried to purchase him, but the livery owner refused.

"He is too big and dangerous for a little lady," he had said every time Lizzie approached him. Being one of the few people who could control Big John, the man's answer had riled her. He never exercised the horse and would not allow her to do it either.

Out of desperation, she asked her husband to go with her. Without even trying to negotiate, Charles handed the man fifty dollars. A fair price for a horse, especially one the livery owner didn't even want.

At eighteen hands, he was considered large, hence the reason for his name. He ate a lot, according to the man, but Charles didn't care. Lizzie wanted him to spend the rest of his life with the care and freedom he deserved.

Charles carried young Oliver to the barn, then reached into his pocket and pulled out several pieces of apple. The smile on his young son's face filled his heart with joy. Big John was far too big for Oliver to ride, and he'd purchased a pony for the boy to learn on.

Lizzie desperately wanted to ride Big John, but in her current state, Charles put his foot down. It didn't stop Lizzie – she had snuck out a few times when he was occupied with their son. The safety of his wife and unborn child were his only concern.

"The horse needs his exercise," she argued. "He won't harm me." Charles was certain her words were true, but didn't want her to take the chance.

Their land was large and sprawling. A small forest was at the end of the acreage, and Lizzie loved to ride there. When it happened, Charles secured Oliver on his pony and held the reins, guiding them along the property.

It was like having a ranch without all the hassle. He wanted to sell the inn and take his family to a ranch outside Helena. Lizzie would have none of it. "The best of both worlds," she told him. After all, the inn was a family business, and he would one day pass it onto his children.

Besides, everyone who worked there was the nearest thing to family they had. How could he break the bond they all shared?

Lizzie was right. She always was, he decided. Charles chuckled at the thought. Where would he be now, he wondered, if she had not sought refuge at the inn? Charles knew the answer without thinking about it.

He would still be that sad man living in his *private quarters*, not his home.

From the Author

Thank you so much for reading my book – I hope you enjoyed it.

I would greatly appreciate you leaving a review where you purchased, even if it is only a one-liner. It helps to have my books more visible!

~*~

About the Author

Multi-published, award-winning and bestselling author Cheryl Wright, former secretary, debt collector, account manager, writing coach, and shopping tour hostess, loves reading.

She writes historical romantic suspense and historical western romance.

She lives in Melbourne, Australia, and is married with two adult children and has six grandchildren, and three great-grandchildren.

When she's not writing, she can be found in her craft room making greeting cards.

$\mathscr{Links}$

Website: http://www.cheryl-wright.com/

Facebook   Reader   Group: https://www.facebook.com/groups/cherylwrightauthor/

Join My Newsletter:

https://cheryl-wright.com/newsletter/
(and receive a free book)

www.ingramcontent.com/pod-product-compliance
Lightning Source LLC
Chambersburg PA
CBHW071019180726
48291CB00004B/1528